Crush du Jour

How NOT to Spend
Your Senior Year
BY CAMERON DOKEY

Royally Jacked
BY NIKI BURNHAM

Ripped at the Seams
BY NANCY KRULIK

Spin Control
BY NIKI BURNHAM

Cupidity
BY CAROLINE GOODE

South Beach Sizzle
BY SUZANNE WEYN AND
DIANA GONZALEZ

She's Got the Beat
BY NANCY KRULIK

30 Guys in 30 Days
BY MICOL OSTOW

Animal Attraction
BY JAMIE PONTI

A Novel Idea
BY AIMEE FRIEDMAN

Scary Beautiful
BY NIKI BURNHAM

Getting to Third Date
BY KELLY McCLYMER

Dancing Queen
BY ERIN DOWNING

Major Crush
BY JENNIFER ECHOLS

Do-Over
BY NIKI BURNHAM

Love Undercover
BY JO EDWARDS

Prom Crashers
BY ERIN DOWNING

Gettin' Lucky
BY MICOL OSTOW

The Boys Next Door
BY JENNIFER ECHOLS

In the Stars
BY STACIA DEUTSCH AND
RHODY COHON

Available from Simon Pulse

Crush du Jour

MICOL OSTOW

Simon Pulse
New York London Toronto Sydney

This book is a work of fiction. Any references to historical events, real people, or real locales are used fictitiously. Other names, characters, places, and incidents are the product of the author's imagination, and any resemblance to actual events or locales or persons, living or dead, is entirely coincidental.

SIMON PULSE
An imprint of Simon & Schuster Children's Publishing Division
1230 Avenue of the Americas, New York, NY 10020
Copyright © 2007 by Micol Ostow
All rights reserved, including the right of reproduction in whole or in part in any form.
SIMON PULSE and colophon are registered trademarks of Simon & Schuster, Inc.
Designed by Ann Zeak
The text of this book was set in Garamond 3.
Manufactured in the United States of America
First Simon Pulse edition October 2007
10 9 8 7 6 5 4 3 2 1
Library of Congress Control Number 2007928438
ISBN-13: 978-1-4169-5027-1
ISBN-10: 1-4169-5027-3

For my father,
who worships Paul Prudhomme

Prologue

My mother always tells me not to bite off more than I can chew.

"You run yourself ragged, Laine," she says. "You've got too much on your plate."

She's wrong.

I've got an appetite for achievement, fine. That much I'll give her. But these days, that's par for the course. I mean, college applications are up by, like, a million percent. It's a cutthroat competition. It used to be that your GPA or test scores were the most important aspect of your candidacy, but now they're just the appetizer, or a playful sort of *amuse-bouche*. You've got to bust your butt on extracurricular activities and knock it out of the park with your interview and essay questions. And if you happen to score well on an advanced placement exam or two? Well, that's merely the icing on the cake.

If I sound like a girl obsessed, there's a reason. My parents split when I was little, and when it comes to tuition, it's really just Mom and me footing the bill. And while my mother's got a great job as the chief restaurant critic for the *Philadelphia Tribune*, we're not exactly millionaires. I need to qualify for financial aid if I'm going to go somewhere other than Penn State.

Talk about type A, right? A junior in high school, and my cups—and my transcripts—already runneth over. Between AP courses, SAT prep, extracurricular activities, and part-time jobs, I don't have a lot of free time. But, you know, if you can't stand the heat, get out of the kitchen.

I can stand the heat. Trust me, my life sometimes feels like one major pressure cooker.

My mom would love it if I spent this summer at the pool club with my best friend, Anna, who's working as an au pair for a Cabana Club couple, flirting with boys, and lazing in a lounge chair. That's what I did the last three summers, despite being highly allergic to sun. Anna and I had a good time—no, make that a *great* time—but times have changed.

But maybe I was having a little too much fun. When it comes to boys, I guess I have sort of a love-'em-and-leave-'em reputation. I can't help it: I see a cute guy and I immediately go all mushy. It's a disease. But now that we're revving up for senior year, it's time to get serious. I'm way too busy to let a guy distract me. No matter how yummy he is. I mean, I do date, but it's never anything serious. I reserve my seriousness for college planning and all things related. Crushes are just a tasty little candy bowl to dip into when I'm running low on spice in my life. Or, if my life is a giant sugar cookie, then crushes are the rainbow sprinkles on top. If life is like a pizza, then crushes are the pepperoni topping. If life is . . . a cheeseburger, then crushes are a side of fries.

You get the point. I may like my french fries (and I do), but they're never going to take the place of a solid main course.

I know some girls think I have my priorities mixed up. And I've been called a tease by some of the boys I've dated, boys who wanted to be more than a side dish in the menu of my life. But college isn't just a pie-in-the-sky fantasy, and as I'm constantly reminding Anna, too many cooks spoil the broth.

My life, my broth. Boys will have to be back-burnered.

For now.

One

You're probably wondering why I pepper my vocabulary with so many cooking puns. (*Pepper!* Ha!) Or maybe you're curious as to why I'm named Laine. The answer to both of those questions is sort of the same.

Laine Harper. That's me. My mother—clearly hallucinating on the aftereffects of some major drugs—named me after her favorite restaurant in New York City, the one that inspired her to worship food enough to want to write about it, extolling its many tasty virtues.

That's right—I'm named after Elaine's, the scary Upper East Side outpost that caters to the Manhattan literati.

I don't care how fancy the place is—I'm

named after a *restaurant*. Don't try to tell me that's not weird. I have no idea how she got my father to go along with this lunacy.

I suppose it could have been worse. I could have been called Emeril.

Whatever. The point is, Mom was off critiquing haute Philadelphia eateries and Dad was just, well, off. I was all alone. Had been for quite some time.

Being on her own, a girl develops some hobbies. Early on, while Mom was playing Iron Chef judge, I was left with little to rely on beyond my own grilled-cheese-making skills. Around age eleven, I dragged out my childhood Easy-Bake Oven and experimented with my own creations, like Easy-Bake quiche and Easy-Bake biscuits. Some projects were more successful than others, but an artist knows that mastery of the craft requires a willingness to take risks.

These days, I was well beyond cooking with a twenty-watt lightbulb. I wasn't exactly Emeril, but I knew my way around the kitchen. If I hadn't taught myself the basics, I probably would have starved to death ages ago. The fancy cookies that Mom brings home from some of her restaurants are *so* never enough to keep a growing girl coasting through the late stages of puberty.

That simply wouldn't do.

Obviously, cooking was two parts survival tactic, one part yet another garnish on my college applications. I'd even figured out a way to turn something that most people saw as a carefree hobby or just a chore into yet another fascinating Thing About Me that would distinguish me from the hordes of other qualified students madly rushing forward with their own collegiate agendas.

While Anna and our other friends squeezed in tanning sessions around diaper duty at the Cabana Club, I was going to be leading a cooking workshop for preteens at the local community center.

Or so I hoped; I still had to actually audition for the gig. But, I mean, come on. It was a done deal. This job was right up my alley. I'd been babysitting for neighbors' kids for the past few years, so I had plenty of experience with kids. And, while I admit that my style in the kitchen can best be described as . . . whimsical, I would think whimsy would be a quality that my supervisor— and my students—would appreciate. Any monkey can follow a recipe. But being able to improvise in the kitchen? To think on your feet? *That* takes some serious skill.

Bravery, too. A heaping spoonful of bravery. And maybe a dash of foolhardiness as well. Then blended together slowly, left to simmer over a low flame, and eventually served at room temperature.

Bon appétit!

The good thing about Anna being at the pool all day was that, as much as I missed our gossip sessions, she wasn't around to distract me. I needed to focus and practice in the kitchen if I was going to wow the people at the rec center enough to get the job. Mom's name carried a certain amount of weight, but it wasn't, like, a given that the position was mine. To be honest, I was really into my practice sessions, and I quickly fell into a comfortable routine of disregarding trivialities like brushing my hair or even changing into actual clothing as I floated through the kitchen well into the early summer evenings.

"Tell me you just changed into your pajamas, and haven't been wearing them all day," my mother said one night when she was unexpectedly blessed to be home by ten.

I couldn't lie to her. I still hadn't even brushed my teeth that day, but somehow, I wasn't embarrassed.

"You should talk," I replied, eyeing her up and down.

The thing about being a food critic is that most of the good chefs in town know exactly who you are, and they brief their staff on your stats—sometimes even going so far as to paste your photo somewhere in the kitchen. This way, everyone can recognize you.

Naturally, when a restaurant critic is recognized, he or she is suddenly given the VIP treatment, which compromises the review.

So Mom came up with her own rules (and by "came up with," I mean "borrowed them from a big *New York Times* critic"). First, she always visits a restaurant three times before she writes up her review. That way, she's got a sense of the average overall performance of the place, and she can judge more fairly.

Second, she retains her anonymity by wearing costumes. There's genius in its simplicity.

Wait—did I say simplicity? I meant simplicity of concept, not execution. Because her costumes are more elaborate than a Vegas showgirl's. I'm not saying that she dresses like a stripper, of course, but when she goes undercover, Mom really goes whole hog.

Today, for instance, she wore her Muriel costume. Muriel looks like a distant relative you see only at Christmas, when she pats you on the head as if you are permanently eight years old and regales you with the details of her latest low-grade health concerns.

There was not a lot of vanity involved in becoming Muriel, so I felt that my mom had earned my arched eyebrow. No matter how many times I saw her dressed up—and believe me, it was a lot of times—the success of her transformation always took me by surprise.

She rolled her eyes right back at me. "I'll have you know that Muriel very much enjoyed her dinner at the Blue Pelican tonight."

"The Blue Pelican? Isn't that the place where they only serve raw foods?" I shuddered. Who in their right mind would leave the house and pay good money to be served food that hadn't even been cooked?

"Yes, it is, and believe it or not, the food was outstanding. I had a lasagna made from pureed zucchini."

I made another face, this one gaggier, with sound effects. "I like my pasta made with pasta, thank you," I told her.

"Don't knock it till you've tried it," my mom insisted. She paused, finally starting to take in the disaster zone of the kitchen, and slowly shook her head.

"Laine," she said, "what exactly happened in here?"

I smiled sheepishly. "I had a fight with some slow-simmered tomatoes, and the tomatoes won."

While my mom was out eating "lasagna" made out of sliced squash, I'd been home creating a carbo-loaded lasagna masterpiece with actual noodles that needed no sarcastic air quotes. Yes, the kitchen was a tad bit messy. But whatever. The sauce had been divine. And everybody knows that if you want to make an omelet, you have to break some eggs.

"I see," she replied drily. "I suppose this house is going to be a disaster zone until you have your interview?"

"Uh-huh. And probably even after that. If I get the job, I'm still going to have to test recipes at home, you know?"

"Just try not to demolish the kitchen. *Please?*" She sighed.

"Would I do that to you?" I asked.

"Do you really need me to answer that?" she shot back. She gestured limply to the carnage that surrounded us, making sure to point out some dried chopped spinach crusted onto the front left hip of my pajama pants.

"I have no interest in disasters," I assured her. Rogue chopped spinach notwithstanding, of course. "This was more like a minor tremor."

Yeah, so it turns out? Cooking a lasagna? Can be tricky.

I hated to play out my mother's worst expectations of me. And yet, in my attempt to become the teen Mario Batali, I somehow managed to coat every available kitchen surface in spatters of tomato (marinara sauce from scratch), cooking spray (to prevent sticking), and—I really have no idea how this happened—a thin crust of ricotta-spinach mixture that was rapidly hardening into a stubborn paste. Scraping away at it with a butter knife, I had to entertain the possibility that I might never be able to restore the kitchen to its previous state of order. That was going to be a problem.

"Forget the cleaning for right now," my mother said kindly.

"Thanks."

"I think we're going to have to buy some of those special Brillo pads if we really want to make a dent in this mess," she added.

Right. *"Thanks,"* I sniffed, slightly offended. "Keep in mind, Mom, that a good meal is like a work of art," I reminded her.

She wrinkled her forehead skeptically. "Hence your decision to transform my kitchen into a Jackson Pollock."

"It'll be fine." I waved my hand dismissively. "And as you always say, traditionally, the kitchen was the heart of the family." I batted my eyelashes at her beatifically. "I was just trying to bring a little more heart into our home."

Mom almost had an aneurysm trying to stifle her laughter.

"Mock me all you want," I said, spooning up a bite of my masterpiece for her. "We'll see who has the last laugh."

Mom convulsed, chortling, all over

again, but she did somehow manage to extend her fork with a shaky hand and shovel up a healthy bite. "H-h-ot," she said, waving her hand in front of her mouth.

"Yes, steam does generally indicate heat," I said, quickly pouring her a glass of ice water. I really wasn't looking to destroy her taste buds. For one thing, her taste buds were kind of our livelihood. For another, well, that just wouldn't be very nice. And she was being a pretty good sport about the condition of the kitchen.

She chewed thoughtfully for a moment. I watched her curiously—I'd be lying if I said I wasn't looking for some sort of validation. She swallowed very deliberately and took a long sip of her water.

After a moment of watching her Adam's apple bob up and down, my floss-thin thread of patience disintegrated. "What do you think?" I asked.

She cocked her head at me. "Did I taste pesto in there?" she asked.

I nodded proudly. "Homemade. I added it to the cheese and spinach to give it a little kick."

"Huh," she said, as though she'd never considered that before. Maybe she hadn't.

I mean, even restaurant critics hadn't tasted every single food in the world, right? I mean, that would be, like, a lot of food.

She smiled at me warmly. "What a great idea," she said. "I love it."

"Enough to forgive me for trashing the kitchen?" I asked.

She narrowed her eyes at me. "Don't push your luck, Laine."

Over the next few days, I put my culinary skills to the test. After all, I'd need to be in top form if I wanted to wow the folks at the rec center. I dug out old recipe books (in perfect shape, since my mother rarely cooked), and slogged my way through them, trying to add my own twist here and there when I could. Sure, there were a few missteps. My enchiladas with mole sauce, for example, were more like enchiladas with mole cement. I had to call for an emergency backup pizza that night. And when I tried to make chocolate chip cookies with white chocolate chips, the entire batch came out so sweet that I nearly went into sugar shock. My goal was to figure out both what I enjoyed cooking most and what I was best at cooking. The interview was Saturday morning, and I wanted to be 107 percent prepared.

Gradually, I progressed from simpler dishes like pastas and casseroles to more elaborate, elegant fare, like pan-seared lamb chops and pureed parsnip and leeks. And, other than a *tiny* misunderstanding regarding the Cuisinart (Who knew that the plastic thingy had to be securely fastened to the top of the machine when in use?), nothing that I made really seemed all that toxic or dangerous if ingested. I was growing and stretching and learning, which I felt made me the perfect candidate to teach little kiddies how to spruce up their PB and J sandwiches.

I was putting the finishing touches on a goat-cheese tempura salad one evening when my mother walked through the front door.

"The place smells amazing," she called from the foyer. "What are you making?"

I dashed to meet her. "It's a salad. Fried goat cheese. But it's for one," I admitted guiltily. "You said you weren't coming home."

"Muriel was supposed to visit Hype, that new place off Rittenhouse Square that's billing itself as 'eclectic.'"

Mom shivered. She always says that restaurant critics learn to be wary of terms like "eclectic" or "fusion." Both are trends that can easily veer off course in the hands of a less skilled professional. "But the opening was delayed by a week."

I sucked my breath in quickly. The only thing potentially worse than amateur fusion cuisine is a much-delayed restaurant opening. "Wylie Dufresne is the only man who can get away with that," was my mother's mantra (he's some big-time New York City chef).

"Unfortunate," was all I could muster.

"Tell me about it," Mom said. She hung her coat up in the hall closet and followed me back into the kitchen. She stuck a finger experimentally into a hunk of goat cheese tempura.

"Excuse me," I growled at her playfully. "Has someone forgotten her manners?"

"Your texture is perfect," Mom said approvingly. "And it's not too greasy. Well done."

Okay, then. If she was going to compliment my cooking, then I'd let her poke at my cheese all she wanted.

"I think there's some leftover lentil soup from last week in the freezer," I said. "Why don't we heat that up, and we can split the salad as a first course?"

"Now you're talking," Mom agreed. "I'm so glad that I taught you to share." She opened up a cabinet and pulled down place settings for the both of us. She smiled at me. "Table for two."

TWO

"So, on a scale of one to ten, how prepared are you for the rec center interview?" Mom asked, pausing for a moment from scarfing down her half of our salad.

"Fourteen," I said. I winked at her.

"I worry sometimes about your self-esteem." Mom grinned, so I knew she was joking.

"Yeah, I've got too much of it. But the thing is, I've been practicing in the kitchen for weeks now. And I've done up a bunch of sample menus. I mean, there's no way I'm not qualified for the gig. I just have to charm the interviewer. Make her want me more than any other qualified candidate."

"Who's the interviewer?"

I shrugged. "Nora something. The info is written down somewhere in my bedroom. I've been trying to save my mental energy for the interview itself."

"Fair enough," my mother said. "Just as long as you give her actual name as much study attention as your whole spiel."

"I will, I promise." I took a sip of Diet Coke. "I have to get this job. It's one of the only gigs I could find that would look good on a college transcript that also pays cold, hard cash." I wasn't too proud to admit it; the money actually meant something to me. Most counselor-y sorts of positions were either volunteer or so low-paid that they might as well have been volunteer.

"You know," Mom began casually, "the Lifestyles section has a pretty tight relationship with the community center. I could probably put in a call—"

I groaned. "Not necessary. I don't need any favors." Besides, my last name spoke volumes as it was. Everyone knew about my mother. I figured it was classier to let my family tree speak for itself, rather than to call in a favor.

"Fine with me," my mother said. "It just

so happens that I've got some friends on the Halliday board."

Halliday is shorthand for the Miles Halliday Community Center. I have no idea who Miles Halliday was, but in addition to a community center, he also at some point seems to have funded a library, a town hall, and a community pool just outside Philly. The last time I'd been to the community center was for gymnastic lessons. I was seven.

"'Friends on the board?' Are you part of some sort of Philadelphia culinary mafia?"

She waved her hand at me impatiently. "Sweetie, I know that you're great in the kitchen, but for this job, you need to be great with kids, too."

I stared at her in disbelief. "You don't think the Robinsons would vouch for me?" I'd au paired for them for the past three summers—at the Cabana Club, as a matter of fact.

"*I* know that you're great with kids. I'm just saying that it wouldn't hurt for the folks at Halliday to know too."

"Hence the References section of the job application," I reminded my mother.

She nodded at me. "Gotcha. You've clearly thought this through."

I gave her a look.

"Not that I'm surprised," she added hastily. "You were born prepared."

Nora Ellwood sounded accommodating enough on the phone, but as it turned out, she and I had very different ideas as to how to interpret the phrase "You can't miss it."

For instance, in reference to her office on the second floor of Halliday, what she obviously meant was, "You'll need a divining rod, a miner's cap, and possibly a bloodhound to find it."

Unfortunately, I had none of those things on me, which meant that at 2:16, fully one minute late for our meeting, I was blindly groping my way out of a supply closet and back into the hallway in the direction of a placard marked ROOMS 220–230.

It was *much* more likely that she was somewhere in rooms 220–230 than in the supply closet. So clearly I had a problem. I stepped back out of the supply closet, unsure of what to do next. I really needed to brush up on my navigational skills.

A face framed in salt-and-pepper curls peeped out from one of the offices that dotted the hallway. "Lost?"

I shook my head vigorously. "No." I blushed. "More like . . . directionally challenged."

She laughed. "Laine Harper?"

"That's me." How humiliating. I hoped she wouldn't hold my deficit sense of direction toward my eligibility for this job.

"Come on in." She waved me toward her.

I followed Nora into her office and seated myself at the proffered chair that sat facing her desk. The room was cluttered, but in a comfortable sort of way. If the place had been big enough for a bed, I could easily have camped out there. Various posters featuring endearing animals and encouraging affirmations adorned the walls alongside dry-erase calendars and multicolored cork boards.

"So, Laine, tell me a little bit about yourself," she began, smiling kindly at me.

I cleared my throat, the thick, gagging sound filling the room awkwardly. "Um, well, I'm sixteen, and I go to Hillsdale Public—not now, obviously, since it's the summer, but during the school year, that's where I go—"

Okay, so I babble when I'm nervous. What of it?

"—and I love to cook, and I love kids. So I think the chance to work with kids and teach them to cook would be the ideal summer job for me." I finished my spiel and almost hiccupped, I was so out of breath. I was going to have to pace myself if I didn't want to hyperventilate. I wasn't exactly screaming professionalism.

Why hadn't I let my mother call in a favor?

"Aha," she said, in a tone that suggested she wasn't quite sure what to make of me. "And it says here that you've been babysitting for the past three years?"

"Yup," I confirmed. "I've done a lot of babysitting. It's all on the application. I have references. The ages were five, eight, and eleven. The kids' ages. Not mine." Obviously.

"Yes, well, these children will be somewhat older," Nora warned me. "The age range for our beginning class is eleven to thirteen."

I couldn't see any real problem with this, so I just blinked involuntarily for a beat and hoped that I was projecting the vibe of a person qualified to teach cooking to a bunch of eleven- to thirteen-year-olds.

"You realize that preteens are often rowdy? That this position requires a lot of responsibility and hard work?" she pressed.

"Hard work is my middle name."

(It's actually Agnes.)

Nora spent what felt like five hours but was probably more like five minutes shuffling a pile of papers around on her desk. It did not look as though there was any rhyme or reason to this shuffling, other than to make me nervous. Which I was. I mean, when *I* stack and restack big reams of recycling around in my bedroom, it's usually to make room for my latest project. No one's employment fate rested on my own semi-obsessive stacking habits. Finally, she seemed to find what she was looking for.

"I understand that your mother is Madison Harper, the chief restaurant critic for the *Tribune*."

"Yes, she was very excited when she heard about this program," I said.

"Well, I imagine that you will be a wonderful fit here," she continued, suddenly peering at me as though I were a gnat under the lens of a ginormous microscope. I couldn't tell whether my mother's job was a good thing or a bad thing. If it got me the teaching gig, then I guessed it was a good thing. But Nora looked as though her personal jury was still out, bubbly though she was.

"Great!" I said, perhaps a shade too enthusiastically. I sat ramrod straight in my chair. I quickly adjusted my posture. I mean, I didn't want to seem *too* desperate or anything, you know?

"I love the idea of teaching latchkey kids to cook for themselves. I was a latchkey kid, you know. So, I mean, I'm pretty familiar with taking basic recipes and jazzing them up a little bit."

That was what was going to set me apart from the other contenders, I decided. My jazziness in the kitchen. Anyone could fry up a grilled-cheese sandwich; it took a special sort of visionary to use a hunk of Gruyère instead of American cheese slices.

"I'm glad to hear it," Nora said. "A few details: The ten-week course runs from mid-June to mid-August. The workshops are held on Saturday afternoons, so you should plan to be working through some of your weekends. We also hold a Fourth of July fund-raiser that's called Fantastic Fourth;

you might have been to one, or heard of it at one point or another. And our summer programming culminates in a carnival that all of our instructors help plan."

I nodded briskly, trying to convey seriousness and responsibility. "I'm a good planner," I offered, fully sincere.

"All that's left, then, is the mock class."

My back went rigid all over again. "Um, huh?" I asked. "Mock what?"

I mean, mock *what*? It was my understanding that I had to walk Nora through a lesson plan; teaching a mock class sounded much more involved. And not a little bit scary.

"The class," Nora repeated patiently. To her credit, she was being very delicate about the fact that I was clearly slow on the uptake. "You'll need to improvise a class for me and your potential partner."

Potential *what*-ner? "Who?"

"Your partner," Nora said. "Who's already been assigned. We just need to get a sense of how the two of you would interact together."

This was starting to make a little bit of sense. Not the kind of sense that I was hoping for, where I'd get the job without having to jump through any major hoops, but, well, you can't exactly have your cake and eat it too.

And what does that even mean, anyway? Of *course* you can have your cake and eat it too. That's the whole point of even having cake to begin with. *Unless* it's a Bundt cake or one of those disgusting fruitcakes with the tiny pieces of chopped nuts that everyone's always trying to unload on each other around Christmastime, and—

Oh, right. The interview.

"That's fine," I lied smoothly. I could always do a little practice session with Anna, who loved it when I went all Rachael Ray on her. "When would we do this?"

She looked at me, puzzled, for a beat. My heart sank. I had a feeling I knew what was coming next.

She smiled at me, perkier than she'd been throughout the interview. "We can do it right now!"

Three

When I wandered into the rec center, I'd had no idea that, if I got this job, I would (1) be working with a partner and (2) be forced to perform in front of said partner before I could officially be offered the job.

And yet.

Here I was, at 2:46 on a Tuesday afternoon, being marched down the hallway at a determined clip, on my way to meet a person, probably the same age as I, whose first impression of me would determine the rest of my summer. Or at least the rest of the day.

Not that I was opposed to working in twos, to be honest. It was just sort of jarring to be told that I'd be paired up with some random who'd been hired ages ago. What if

we hated each other? What if she was someone whose boyfriend I'd actually flirted
with at the Cabana Club once upon a time?
(This has been known to happen.)

What if she liked fat-free ice cream?

I shuddered. The walls were a blur of
finger paintings and fliers about racial
diversity. I was starting to feel dizzy. Just as
I was about to completely pass out, Nora
stopped in front of a set of industrial double
doors and pulled them open.

"Here we are," she said briskly. "The
kitchen."

Holy heck, she really was going to make
me cook.

It was a good thing I was so comfortable
with culinary improv.

Past the industrial doors, the space was
actually a little bit sad. I don't know what I
was expecting, since obviously a community
center wouldn't be tricked out like the set of
Iron Chef, but what I found here amounted
to several long cafeteria-style tables set up
to face a bare-bones facsimile of a kitchen.

However.

Dismal as the kitchen itself may have
been, there was one thing in that room that
was absolutely . . . breathtaking.

It was my would-be partner.

The she was a he.

A very-super-extra-adorable he.

Eat your heart out, Laine.

Even my *brain* thought he was out of my league, that's how adorable he was.

Good grief. How in the name of all that is yummy and fatty and very, very bad for you (e.g., ice cream, cookie dough, and white frosting out of the tub) was I going to be able to audition with this dude evaluating my every move? Nora really should have mentioned his debilitating (to me, that is) level of hotness.

"Laine Harper, this is Seth McFadden."

I sighed dreamily. Even his name was cute.

"Hi, Laine." Seth pushed his squeaky folding chair away from the table and stood to shake my hand.

I quickly rubbed my palms against the front of my jeans to shield Seth from what seemed to be a recent-onset glandular problem.

"Hi." I stuck my hand out and grabbed his. He had a firm handshake, which impressed me. I had a sneaking suspicion that my own handshake was more of a deft impression of overboiled pasta. Everything about Seth was confident and well put together, but not in any kind of aggressive, macho-y way. He was almost perfect, in fact—as near as I could tell. Meanwhile, I was sweaty, scattered, and completely unprepared.

Awesome.

Sweaty, scattered, and unprepared was a familiar sensation. It meant something, beyond the temperature in the room.

It meant I was crushing, hard.

This was totally unacceptable. I had officially sworn off crushes for this summer. (Seriously. Anna made me a plaque on her computer and everything. It was *official*.)

"What are you going to be teaching us today, Laine?" Nora asked sweetly as she pulled out a folding chair of her own and made herself comfortable.

This was it. This was the moment of truth. I had perfect confidence that I could teach a class smoothly enough—if only I could decide what I would be teaching. I had visions of tumbleweeds blowing gently across the landscape of my brain. This was ridiculous. After weeks of playing with sample recipes and experimenting in the kitchen, suddenly the jukebox in my mind read TILT.

Five seconds in the room with a cute guy, and my brain was already mush. Do you see why a crush would be way too distracting? Anyway, how does that saying go? "Fake it until you make it?" That's what I needed to do.

I had it. I took a deep breath and pasted a confident smile on my face. "I've been a latchkey kid since I was eleven," I explained, "and I taught myself how to take basic dishes and spice them up—put my own personal flair on them. That's what I'm going to do with you today!"

I felt not unlike an idiot, speaking to a room full of imaginary eleven-year-olds, but I forged ahead determinedly.

"Anyone can make French onion soup," I continued, "but what about baking and toasting your own croutons?"

Nora cleared her throat and waved her hands at me. "I don't think fresh-baked croutons are very practical," she said. "We don't have a bread machine here, and I don't think you'll have enough time in class to wait for dough to rise."

I nodded shortly. "Check. No bread."

"Seth? What would you choose?"

Seth pursed his lips together, appearing to think the question through. After a moment of concentration, he sat up.

"Well, I think sandwiches are a good way to go for one of the earlier lessons, since they're versatile and also easy. I'd start with cold cuts and cheese. Peanut butter and jelly or other standards can be tricky because of food allergies."

Ooh. I wanted to wipe the smug expression off his face with a butter knife. But he must have been going in the right direction, because Nora was beaming at him like he'd just single-handedly carved a twenty-pound Thanksgiving turkey.

"It's a great idea to start with sandwiches," Nora gushed. I may have been a little slow this afternoon, but as a general rule I was no dummy. She was totally into Seth and thought he was an awesome instructor. That annoyed me. *I* liked to be the teacher's pet. Gross, but true.

"I think week one would be a quick overview of the course, and a refresher on kitchen safety," Seth added smugly. Nora nodded so enthusiastically that I was afraid her head was going to snap off at the base of her neck.

OMG, he was *so* the teacher's pet.

Obviously, sandwiches were not exactly haute cuisine. Technically, sandwiches aren't even cooking. I had to admit, that sort of bugged me a little bit. Nora and Seth seemed really into precision, whereas I was a little bit more about shooting from the hip in the kitchen. My creativity was the most important thing that I could bring to my students' table. And it looked like creativity wasn't what Nora wanted.

But I decided that didn't matter. The goal, for now, was to get the job. After all, I needed the experience, and I needed the money. I may have found a deli sandwich to be a sort of . . . uninspired choice for the class, but I needed to find a way to believe in that sandwich, believe in it to my very core.

And believe in that sandwich I did.

"He really said that? *Kitchen safety?*"

Anna and I were camped out at Scoops, a local ice cream parlor set up like an old-fashioned soda shop. You know, one of those places that spell it with the extra letters:

SODA SHOPPE. Despite the fact that Anna's day job had not gotten any easier since the last time I had seen her, my own dire circumstances made an emergency rehash necessary.

Besides, I was doing most of the talking.

"He really did," I confirmed, slurping forlornly at my root beer float. I narrowed my eyes. "And he disagreed with my choice to teach French onion soup, too. Why, Anna?" I pushed my float away from me and leaned into her, grasping at the collar of her terry-cloth hoodie—"*Why* would someone want to sabotage me that way?"

Anna took a second to pry my vicelike fingers off her person. "I don't know, Laine," she replied, pushing me back. "I wasn't there."

"But you admit that it's weird?" I pressed.

Anna sighed. She knew we weren't going anywhere until she told me what I wanted to hear. "It's weird," she agreed, "unless—"

"No, no 'unless'!" I shrieked. A couple at the booth next to us shot me a look. "No 'unless,'" I repeated, this time at a more reasonable volume. "It's just weird."

"*Unless*," Anna continued firmly, "he wasn't trying to sabotage you. I mean, maybe he just really thinks that cold cuts are the foundation of a healthy latchkey diet."

"He's just hot enough to sell that crazy theory, too." The whole experience had made me extremely flustered and a little bit bitter.

Anna nodded. "That might have something to do with your panic too," she suggested. "The hotness."

I snorted. "Unlikely." She was talking nonsense. I paused for a beat. "How so?" Okay, so I was slightly curious. Can you blame me?

She pushed her long, ash blond hair out of her eyes.

"Well, didn't you swear off cute boys for the summer? Because of how they 'interfere with your concentration'?" She made little quote marks with her fingers.

I grunted noncommittally. Leave it to Anna to use my own words against me. Sometimes it was superannoying to have a best friend who knew me so well.

And as much as I can be a flirt, I wasn't totally psychotic when it came to the opposite sex. I mean, it wasn't that I was so insecure— more like inexperienced. At the tender age of sixteen I'd only had one real boyfriend, and that was at camp a whole two summers ago. I'd also never crushed on anyone as objectively cute as Seth. Not that I have any sort of major facial disfiguration, but Seth was adorable, while I was more . . . quirky. My blunt little bob and pervasive freckles sort of sealed that deal for me. Anyway, all I meant was that Seth was a hottie, and potentially just slightly out of my league. But only *slightly*.

And anyway, it didn't matter. Because I wasn't going to hook up this summer—no matter *which* refugee from a CW dramedy was thrown into my path.

I waited a moment or two for Anna to chime in again, but she seemed pretty focused on her chocolate chip ice cream cookie sandwich, which was slowly dribbling onto the Formica table.

"*Obviously*," I continued, when it became clear that I was losing Anna's semidivided attention, "even if I hadn't made a pact with myself, Seth and I can't date if we're going to be teaching together. That would just be unprofessional."

"Maybe you won't get the job." She licked around the edges of her ice cream sandwich to prevent drippage.

"Thanks," I grumbled.

Not dating this summer was, as Anna pointed out, a rule that I had devised all by myself, for myself. I couldn't go back on it five seconds after the first attractive member of the male species crossed my path.

But Seth was way more than an attractive guy. He oozed cute-itude and exuded charm. He emitted some sort of pheromone that I couldn't help but take note of.

In fact, he was downright *yummy*.

Even if he was a snotty little know-it-all in the kitchen.

I came home from Scoops to an empty household. I wasn't surprised; dinner with Mom was about as frequent as sightings of the Loch Ness Monster (and really, when would you see the Loch Ness Monster in Philly, of all places?). However, as I defrosted myself some turkey meatloaf for dinner, I saw that she had left me a note on the wipe board that we have hung on the fridge.

Nora called. Call her back tonight before six or tomorrow. ☺

My mother wasn't very cutesy—she definitely wasn't the type to engage in excessive use of emoticons—so obviously Nora had said something to my mom when they spoke. Something good, that is.

Something about me getting the job.

Four

"My name is Pete, and I like to eat pizza."

"Hi, Pete!" Like a deranged chorus, Seth and I and the five other students in the class, which Nora had named Stirring Things Up, welcomed one of our own.

Even though the icebreakers were mostly my idea, I still couldn't believe we were doing them. From icebreakers, it was a very slippery slope to trust falls, name games, and quasi-paranormal levitation exercises. The last time I'd been forced to levitate or to pin a name tag to my chest was on my first day of middle school—which made sense, since these kids were all around twelve years old.

And while we're on the subject: Twelve years old? Is pretty old. I mean, we're talking free-thinking, gum-snapping, loud-talking old. This didn't bother me so much, but Seth didn't seem totally comfortable or in control of the room. Against my advice, he'd drawn a skull and crossbones on his own name tag, only scribbling his name underneath quickly after an impromptu visit and a questioning glance from Nora.

I did a quick mental inventory: Pete liked pizza, Marci liked marshmallows, Anthony liked apples, Gretchen liked grapes, Cameron liked cookies (I knew he and I were going to get along just fine), and Barrie liked baked potatoes. That was our class, in an icebreaking nutshell.

Pizza-loving Pete was sort of burly, like a preteen teddy bear. I wanted to scoop him up and feed him as much pizza as he wanted. Marshmallow Marci wore bright pink braces on her gums, which seemed like a deadly match for marshmallows in any form, if you asked me. Anthony was skinny, with ruddy cheeks and spiky hair. He didn't strike me as a wholesome, apple-loving guy, but I could allow him the poetic license. Gretchen was willowy and blond and clearly on the cusp of puberty; if it weren't so unprofessional, I might even have been jealous of her. Cameron could have stepped off the set of a CW dramedy or a Disney musical himself. And Barrie? Well, Barrie was sweet. That is to say, sweet was the beginning and the end of it. I had yet to come up with another descriptor for her. My heart went out to her. Maybe she was just painfully shy.

What did Laine like, you ask? Laine liked lollipops. Seth, apparently, was a big fan of surf and turf, but not, it would seem, of twelve-year-old cooking class students.

I was sort of shocked to arrive at Halliday early that first Saturday morning to find Seth hunched over a table in our classroom, scowling at the aprons Nora had left out for us.

"Are they the wrong size?" I joked. They looked big enough to cover an elephant. I'd definitely have to tie mine around my waist at least three times.

"What? Um, I haven't tried them yet." Seth seemed a little bit embarrassed to be caught daydreaming.

"So, what do you think the kids will be like?" I asked, crossing the room and quickly donning one of the two aprons. Yup, it was huge on me. The lower edges of it grazed the tips of my lime green Pumas, which was a shame, since they were super-cute sneakers and I was really into them. Oh, well. At least I was unlikely to get them dirty.

"I have no idea," Seth said, a blank look in his eyes. He was either terrified of children or had been replaced by a cooking-instructor cyborg.

Nora stopped in to say hello and wish us luck for our first class. That seemed to snap Seth out of whatever little trance he'd gone into, thank goodness, because even though I had experience with kids, I was intimidated by the thought of actually being in charge of a group of them and being responsible for teaching them. Suddenly the kitchen, once my favorite room of any house, seemed fraught with danger. Knives, fire, and big, heavy bags of dry goods? Add those ingredients to a room full of hyper kids and you've got a recipe for disaster.

For all that Seth was flustered when I found him, he pulled himself together for the actual class. That is, he stopped enacting the thousand-yard gaze of terror.

Unfortunately, he hadn't replaced it with anything more authoritative, and as a result, the kids weren't taking him all that seriously. It wasn't an immediate problem, but I sensed that it could morph into one at any moment. It made me very tense.

"Well then," I said, clapping my hands briskly, "should we get started?"

Everyone responded with medium-grade enthusiasm. Something had to be done. I wanted these kids to be super-extra-totally psyched for cooking class.

"People," I said, leaning my hands on the table in front of me and hunching forward conspiratorially, "cooking is *fun*. Your parents sent you to this class so you could learn how to safely mess around in the kitchen while they're at work. Come on—you really don't think that sounds awesome?"

A mild murmur broke out among the group. While they didn't respond with as much enthusiasm as I would have liked, the general feeling was that yes, this sounded somewhat awesome.

Okay, so maybe they weren't exactly raring to go, but I was going to have to seize whatever energy they could muster and go with it. I grinned as widely as I could. ·

"The purpose of this class is to teach you basic kitchen skills and safety. That way you don't have to have Doritos for dinner whenever your parents are working late."

"I *like* Doritos," Anthony interjected, looking skeptical.

I waved an arm at him dismissively.

"I'm not saying you *can't* have chips. My point is only that you can have a real dinner, too."

He nodded, not looking very convinced.

I was in too deep, and I wasn't getting any help from Seth, either. There was nothing left to do but go for broke. "Today," I continued, sounding as perky as a Barbie doll on diet pills, "we're going to *quickly* go over some cooking basics"—I had to rush through this part; it sounded dry even to my own ears—"and then we'll talk about the foundations of healthy eating."

Oh, jeez. Listening to myself, I sort of wanted to curl up with a bag of Doritos myself, which was so unlike me. If I was going to curl up with a snack, it would at least be some air-popped popcorn with some cumin and garlic salt.

"Forget that."

I looked up, startled. I thought it was

Anthony, protesting what could possibly be the most boring extracurricular activity of all time, ever. I was all prepared to tease and cajole him in a way that demonstrated just how cool and with-it I was.

(Note: As a general rule, people who are "cool" and "with it" do not need to use sarcastic quote marks when they describe themselves. But I digress.)

Imagine my surprise when I discovered that it was actually Seth who was undermining my carefully laid-out lesson plan. The lesson plan that I had gone over first with him and then with Nora. The lesson plan that had been—much like every other undertaking in my entire life—*approved*.

I cleared my throat. "I'm sorry?"

Seth looked up. "'Basics' and 'foundations'? Who wants to work on that?"

Well, we did, according to the conversation that we had had, um, *yesterday*.

"How about we do something fun? How about we head into the pantry and MacGyver up some macaroni and cheese? Bonus points for figuring out how to add something extra weird to the mix."

"Marshmallows?" Marci asked hopefully.

Seth flushed brightly, still somewhat

terrified by the room full of twelve-year-olds. It was becoming crystal clear to me that we were total opposites. I was a planner—except with food—and good with kids. He was a "winger"—except in the kitchen, where he fell back on total basics—and, apparently, was crap with kids. But if we each had our own special skill set, why was he going all improv on me when I least expected it? Was he trying to throw me off of my game?

Together, we either made the awesomest, most perfect teaching team ever . . . or we were going down in flames.

We'd just have to wait and see.

For now, I decided, it didn't matter. We could be a modern-day Hepburn and Tracy, or better yet, Nick and Jessica pre-divorce. Except, without the romance. And with slightly smaller bank accounts. And—at least as far as I was concerned—less shiny hair. Not that Seth was noticing my hair, anyway.

We were clearly, completely, one hundred percent polar opposites. And not the kind that attracted.

Unfortunately.

In the meantime, however, it seemed we

were going to be jumping headfirst into a macaroni-and-marshmallow casserole.

Yum.

That night dinner was a warmed-over Tupperware container of sticky grated cheddar and rigatoni, mixed with medium-spicy salsa left over from the week before. I was either going to gain ten pounds or die of malnutrition while I taught this class—possibly even both. Mom and I had resorted to communicating almost strictly through the wipe board on the refrigerator since we had practically ceased to see each other in person. In the foodie business summer was all about seasonal specials and garden openings. Tonight, Mom's note said, she was on her way to that new place Hype for her first visit. She was going dressed as Laurel, a savvy media professional who is all business, all the time. (Laurel looks a lot like my mom wearing a blond wig.)

"I hope it lives up to all the 'hype,'" she wrote.

I winced at the awful pun. No matter how mediocre Hype turned out to be, she'd still have it better than I did. I checked my watch: I'd given myself thirty minutes of downtime before I dove into some SAT flash cards. I planned to use those thirty minutes to full advantage. I curled up to the television with my plate of pasta and settled in for an *Iron Chef America* mini-marathon.

Five

"So, is Seth still babelicious?" Anna's green eyes peered at me inquisitively from behind the world's biggest Slushee. She was being a good friend, listening to me mope about a cutie I couldn't have, rather than regaling me with torrid tales of the beach club. That Anna—she's a thoughtful wingman. Or wingwoman.

I nodded morosely. *"Muy caliente."*

She was puzzled. "Then why do you look like he kidnapped your puppy?"

I stared at her. "Do we *really* need to go over this again?"

Obviously, we did. I sat straight up in my chair, my order of atomic wings pushed aside and neglected.

"One," I began, ticking my points off sequentially on my sauce-sticky fingers, "we are complete and total opposites. No, we're beyond opposites. Opposites are things that don't match. We've got some kind of weird chemistry where if we were thrown together into a bowl, we'd cause an explosion."

"That's where you lose me. 'Cause, see, explosive chemistry? Is usually considered a good sign."

Hmm. Anna might have had a point there, actually. I was starting to regret agreeing to meet her at the diner. Seth and I could *not* get together, which was a resolution that I needed Anna to help me keep. Because I sure didn't trust myself to do it on my own.

Seth *was* babelicious. He was crunchy and yummy and covered in sprinkles with a cherry on top. I wanted to devour him—in a totally appropriate, nonsexual way, of course.

"Do you or do you not remember the oath I took at the beginning of the summer?"

"You were going to grow your bangs out," Anna offered. She pointed to her own forehead. "That inspired me to cut new ones."

Well, that too. I was having about as much success with my bangs as I was not-crushing on Seth.

"Okay, yeah, the bangs, sure. But also, I swore off boys. Remember? No more crush of the days. Or is it crushes of the day?" I scrunched my face up, puzzling out the sentence.

"Don't tell me you're going to get obsessed about grammar now as well." Anna rolled her eyes.

"I'm serious." She was starting to exasperate me. "Not about the grammar, or whatever. But—next year we're seniors. After first semester, our academic fates are totally sealed. This is my last chance to piece together the perfect application. This cooking class needs to run smoothly." If only I could run my whole summer through a Cuisinart.

Anna nodded. It looked like I was starting to get through to her. "Which means no distractions."

"Exactly!" I slapped the table enthusiastically, causing Anna's Slushee cup to tip slightly. Sludgy goodness spilled all over the place.

"I hear what you're saying, Laine, and you know I want to support you," she said.

"But?"

"But." She sighed. "You going a whole

summer with a red-hot romance of the superficial variety? On a scale between one and unlikely?"

I glared at her. Using my history against me was *so* cheap.

"Well, let's just say that my Slushee has more of a chance of being added to the USDA food pyramid than you do of getting over your Seth-love without even a tasty little fling."

"Back burner," I told her, tapping the tabletop authoritatively. "Love is on the back burner. For now."

"Maybe it shouldn't be," she offered. Unlike me, Anna was a serial monogamist. She rarely went more than a few weeks between boyfriends, which meant she was due for a new one any day now.

"Romance is a good thing, you know. Or it can be."

"So should I ask Seth to dance by the dry-goods pantry?"

"Funny. Look, you keep saying that you don't want to crush on Seth, and that's fine, I get that. But what if you actually had an actual relationship? Unlike crushes, relationships can be less distracting and more supportive."

I raised an eyebrow at her. "If I wanted more support, I'd buy a new sports bra. You're all the support I need for right now."

She snorted. "We'll see." She waggled a finger at me knowingly. "Just keep in mind, some hotties have a shelf life. If you spend your summer slaving in the kitchen, when you're finally ready to flirt again . . . Seth may be off the menu."

According to Mom, Hype was, in fact, mostly hype, though she still had two more visits to go before she'd write her review. As for my cooking class, we were chopping away fiendishly, but as for actual cooking? Not so much.

I couldn't believe how much my painstakingly rendered lesson plans were being changed. I'd been so enthusiastic about jazzing up simple basics, but the reality was that the students? Not so much. They weren't interested in subbing fondue for grilled cheese or prosciutto with melon for bologna sandwiches. They were, well, just kids, when it came down to it. And they may have loved me, but they also loved Seth's cooking.

It was so strange. We were like those old

commercials for Reese's Peanut Butter Cups: "Two great tastes that taste great together." I was the peanut butter; I had the rapport and the experience with kids. Seth was the chocolate; he could barely make eye contact with the kids, but he knew what they liked. And it wasn't fondue or fancy salami.

Obviously, I knew that we were supposed to cater to the kids on their own level; after all, this class was really about giving them the tools they needed to feed themselves well, safely, and healthily while their parents were at work. But did that really mean we had to resort to things like prepackaged sponge cake and canned fruit salad? I just wanted to inject some imagination or sophistication into these dishes— but no one else was having it.

While I stood in the corner silently fretting, Seth and the rest of the class were draining and rinsing canned beans for a vegetarian three-bean chili. I had lobbied for soy crumbles in the mix, but I'd been outvoted. Apparently, some kids are grossed out by soy. Who knew?

Rinsing beans is a soggier business than most people realize. Droplets of bean juice ran out of the sink and onto the tiled floor.

Seth inched over to my workspace and poked me in the ribs. "Do you think we should put a stop to that?" He jerked his head in the direction of Pete and Barrie, who were the sous-chefs involved in primary bean drainage. Barrie grappled with the electric can opener while Pete struggled to get the faucet sprayer under control. The little hose had been turned to maximum output and was now waving about like the tentacles on an octopus. Pete looked like he was rehearsing the upside-down kiss in *Spider-Man*—his hair was drenched and plastered to his cheeks.

I shrugged. "They're standing on the paper." We laid paper out before the class and tossed it in the garbage at the end of the day.

"But we're the ones who have to clean up the paper, ultimately," Seth pointed out.

It was annoying when someone so cute could be so reasonable. The last five minutes of every class were dedicated to clean-up time, but it wasn't the kids' top skill. That was okay with me, though, because I had a secret: I liked staying behind afterward, tidying up with Seth.

That was cool, wasn't it? It was a nice, nonromantic way to spend time with him that didn't violate any previously established solemn oaths. Meanwhile, he probably thought I was just a big type A who couldn't leave until every fleck of baking soda was restored to its rightful space in the pantry.

I could live with that.

As much as I enjoyed our housekeeping sessions together, Seth was right: Cleaning up after the students was a huge pain in the butt.

"Remind me again why we didn't make Barrie and Pete do this," he huffed while scraping away at a bean that someone had ground into the floor tiles with particular aplomb.

I shuddered. "Honestly? I really don't trust them to do a thorough job. And we're the ones on the line if we trash the kitchen," I said. *I am nothing if not matter-of-fact about my control issues, if a little bit euphemistic about it,* I thought.

"Besides," I continued, "the nicer we are to them, the bigger the tips from their parents at the end of the summer." Yeah, it was a paid gig, but as teachers, our base salaries were laughably low. Halliday wasn't exactly flush with cash. I was counting on tips from satisfied parentals to supplement my college fund.

Seth looked up from his bean mission. "Tips?"

"Um, yeah. You know, like you get at camp," I said, wondering if I had somehow lapsed into a different language or something.

I have to admit, the expression on Seth's face worried me. But then, it was obvious that he hadn't spent much time around kids. So maybe it made sense that he was a tip virgin.

"Uh, Laine," he said, sounding a little bit like my mom had when she'd broken the news to me that our cat, Itsy, had run away, "didn't Nora tell you? The parents aren't allowed to tip. It's Halliday policy."

My stomach dropped. I wanted to faint.

No, wait—I wanted to *scream*.

Not allowed?

Policy?

What sort of lunatic policy was that?

Well, okay, it was obviously the sort of lunatic policy that went toward making sure certain kids didn't get special treatment. Obviously, I knew that much. But

Nora had clearly forgotten to share this little tidbit of information with me.

I mean, I like to think I would have taken the job anyway. After all, the community center was a great city resource, and it was important that we support it. And the cooking class was something that college admissions boards would eat up (no pun intended), especially since I come from a culinary background. But that didn't change the fact that a journalist's salary and student loans only went so far. And I'd really been counting on those tips.

I sighed, forlorn. My money woes were slowly turning me into a glass-half-empty sort of girl.

"I wish someone had told me that *before* I'd decided to blow off working at the swim club for the summer."

Poor, poor me. And to think, I was missing out on all the adorable lifeguards as well. Swearing off boys suddenly seemed like a terrible idea: Why deprive myself of one of life's few real joys?

I had made a huge mistake.

Seth tied off the enormous black garbage bag he'd been wrestling with. "You need a job?" he asked with interest.

"'Need' is a very subjective word," I

replied, "but yes, now that you mention it, my bank account could use some subsidizing."

"Why don't you come work for me?" Seth offered.

Yeah, more time with the boy I was lusting after—whom I wasn't supposed to be lusting after. That sounded like a good idea. *Not.* Crushing was one thing, but at this point Seth and I were too close for comfort. Getting involved with him would be stickier than a Cinnabon.

He smiled encouragingly. "The tips are great."

Well, see, now he had me. But what would working for him entail, especially seeing as how tips were involved? "Say more."

"It's just, we might be able to help each other out. Can you wait?"

I frowned. Waiting was not one of my strong suits. I think the patience fairy skipped me back when I was born.

"Um, I think sometimes I can get carried away," I said apologetically, "and then I get impatient—"

"What?" Seth looked bewildered. "What does getting carried away have to do with being a waitress?"

Oh, he was talking about *waiting*, waiting. Cool. That made a lot more sense.

"That makes more sense," I said out loud.

"Yeah." Seth nodded, obviously not understanding my thought process at all. See? Oscar and Felix. Oil and water. Buffy and vampires. We had the bad, explosive kind of chemistry.

If only he wasn't so freaking cute.

"My dad's in a bind, and we didn't know what we were going to do. He's down one server, and so far, there are no prospects on the horizon—I think because the summer is so busy for restaurants."

Didn't I know it. I hadn't seen my mother since Memorial Day.

"Your dad runs a restaurant?" I was a little bit late to the party, which was affecting my level of comprehension.

Sean laughed. "How do you think I got this gig without any previous teaching experience? My dad owns a restaurant. A new one. You might have heard of it." With a grunt, he tossed the last garbage bag onto a pile by the front door, for the janitors to pick up later.

A sinking feeling settled in my stomach, like I'd made the mistake of riding the

Ferris wheel after three too many cotton candies. "Um, maybe," I said weakly, worried about what he'd say next.

"It's called Hype," he finished. "We just opened. We're still waiting for the top reviews to come in." He glanced at me curiously, as though thinking of something for the first time.

"Hey," he said easily, "what do *your* parents do?"

★

Me: Hey, Mom, are you busy?

Mom: Sort of, sweetie. We're on deadline, and the managing editor is literally standing over me, waiting for my piece.

Me: Really? Um, okay, I'll make this fast. I mean—what piece are you working on?

Mom: You remember, Hon—that rock-and-roll sushi karaoke joint that I tried to convince you to visit with me.

Me: Right, that one. Pity I'm not more of a karaoke type. But, uh, you never told me what you thought of Hype.

Mom: Oh, boy. *Really* not worth mentioning. The service was unimpressive—

Me: Well, you know, I mean, maybe they're short staffed or whatever right now.

Mom: Huh. Maybe. But beyond that, the food was very uneven, mediocre at best. They're going to have to step it up if they want to compete with the restaurants in this town.

Me: *(slightly panicked gasping noise)*

Me: *(after calming down)* Right, but, um, are you going to pan them in the *Tribune*?

Mom: *(hearty laughter)* Of course not!

Me: *(under my breath)* Oh, thank freaking goodness.

Mom: After all, they get two more chances to change my mind.

Right.

One minute I was a mildly neglected latchkey kid who had a string of crushes and an empty piggy bank. Now, suddenly, I had two jobs that, frankly, I wasn't all that good or experienced at, and one *huge* crush that seemed completely ill advised. Even worse, I was living a lie.

Okay, maybe that's putting it a little bit melodramatically. I'm not a manipulative mastermind, after all. But like it or not, I *was* working the art of misdirection.

For instance, since my mother never outright asked if I was working as a waitress at one of the newest, most overhyped (in her opinion, anyway) restaurants in town, I didn't bring it up with her. And when Seth asked me what my parents do for a living, I talked my absentee father up, big-time. I told him my mom was "a foodie," which was just vague enough not to be a lie.

Suddenly my calendar was looking like a five-course meal. And it was only going to get worse. I had to hope that my appetite held up.

Six

The thing about being an uptight, overly scheduled, hyperorganized sort of person is that sometimes you kind of come across like a butt-kissing geek.

I, for instance, was so wired for my first day as a waitress at Hype that I'd arrived a full thirty minutes early for my shift. It was a tad embarrassing; Seth had told me to come "a little bit" ahead of time so that I could get the tour and other orientation sort of information and stuff. Still, there's a yawning chasm between "a little bit" and thirty minutes. Thank goodness Seth didn't know the full, actual truth: that I'd popped straight up in bed at seven fifteen that morning only to sit, pretty much motionless in that position, until my alarm went off two hours later. That's how nervous I was about my first evening shift at Hype.

Sometimes even I am horrified by the depths of my own dorkiness.

When I arrived at the restaurant, everyone appeared to be in a full predinner swing. Waiters and waitresses sat quietly at a table in the back of the main dining room, methodically rolling place settings up in freshly pressed cloth napkins. Busboys replenished the sideboards with salt, pepper, and other condiment-y stuff.

The space itself was what you might expect for a sophisticated urban eatery: long, slim, mod wood tables stained dark, ultra-angular chairs covered in bright, contrasting fabric. Square sconces dotted the walls, creating a quiet but elegant mood. I could see why this place would be popular among Philadelphia's young professionals.

I only hoped that Philadelphia's young professionals were generous tippers.

"Laine! You found the place!"

Seth's face popped into frame just in front of me. Startled, I tried not to jump. I didn't want Seth to think that his face was unwelcome in my personal space.

"Your directions were great. And also, I live nearby."

I lived right near Seth's father's restaurant. It was like we were destined to date. Seriously, the universe was practically throwing us into each others' paths.

I needed to have a frank heart-to-heart with the universe, stat. I had to inform the universe of my pledge of a crush-free summer, and the fact that my mother and Seth's father were sworn, if unknown, enemies. The universe was making things very difficult for me, after all.

Seth's eyes twinkled at me, taking me in. Those were some sparkly eyes. Almost hypnotic, even. He was looking better and better to me every time I saw him. In fact, I was starting to develop the sneaking suspicion that if and when Seth and I did get together, it would be way more of a main-course sort of deal, rather than an appetizer. This only made things more complicated.

Maybe I could talk to the universe in, say . . . September? You know, have one last, crush-tastic fling with Seth and then buckle down for my senior year. That wasn't asking too much, was it?

I guessed that it wasn't—as long as what happened with Seth *was* truly a fling. And that seemed less and less likely the more I got to know him.

Focus, I commanded myself. Yes, it was a shame that my tendency to jump from crush to crush faster than Lindsay Lohan changes hair color was totally at odds with my otherwise buttoned-up personality. But I did have some shred of self-control. I wasn't completely at the mercy of my hormones. And right now, the promise of cold, hard cashola was slightly more appealing than Seth's chiseled cheekbones.

Only slightly, but still. Slightly was something.

There he went with the smiling again. Dimples erupted right and left. Seth and the universe must have been in cahoots.

"C'mon," he said, clapping a hand on my shoulder and beckoning me toward the kitchen. "I'll show you around."

If Seth thought I was weird or high-strung for showing up to work so early, then he must have thought I was completely, full-blown bonkers once I was tossed into the pit with the rest of the Hype waitstaff.

In theory, my working at Hype was the best possible solution for everyone. Obviously, I needed to make some extra cash, and Seth's father was downright desperate for a warm body to cover tables three through seven. Voilà! Two birds, one stone, problem solved.

But that's a lot of tables, three through seven. Especially for someone who's never worked in a restaurant before. I was in over my head before my first official shift even began.

First, there was the issue of the Hype uniform, of which I'd been blissfully unaware until now. I'd changed outfits at least sixty-three times before I left for the restaurant (in fact, trying on every single combination of outfits in my closet had been my single most aggressively pursued pastime, once I actually got out of bed). I needed something professional but comfortable. Something clean and simple—but something that might actually make me look pretty if, for instance, Seth or . . . someone else happened to notice me.

I know, I know—I wasn't supposed to be caring about the opposite sex. But you can't teach an old dog new tricks, right? Old habits die hard.

Seth walked me through the restaurant and introduced me to the rest of the staff. I was informed that the kitchen staff was really the lifeblood of the place and that it was important to stay on their good side. The manager on schedule for that night was hiding away in his basement office, taking advantage of the early-evening lull to tackle some paperwork. The only people whose names I could remember were Damien, the bartender, and Callie, a waitress who'd been with Hype since the grand opening—and who definitely didn't seem to appreciate my coming on board.

I had just launched into an inner monologue in which I congratulated myself for being so cool and collected (and perfectly accessorized) in front of my new coworkers, when Seth dropped a minibomb on me.

"You're going to have to get dressed."

I did a panicked assessment of myself. Had I actually left the house naked? That would have been crazy ironic if I'd left the house naked after trying on every single outfit I owned. I patted my legs and was relieved to feel them covered in the soft cotton of my lucky plaid skirt. I was being insane. For real. I mean, Damien would have looked at me a whole lot differently if I'd been unclothed when we were introduced. He was a flirt with a capital *F*, like me. I just knew it, even after the innocuous "hey" we'd greeted each other with.

What can I say? I have a special radar for cute boys who could potentially keep up a steady chatter of innuendo-laden banter. It's a gift, like the way Anna can solve geometric proofs in her sleep.

"How do you mean?" I asked.

"Your uniform," Seth explained. "Everyone wears black polo shirts and black pants." He waved a hand up and down his front to demonstrate his own compliance with this rule. He also wore a bright red apron with lots of little pockets for pen and paper that I assumed was also part of the required outfit.

"I, uh, didn't bring mine."

Seth laughed. "I should have told you—we've got a set for you. At least, they *should* fit. What size are you?"

Clearly, Seth had no idea that asking a girl what clothing size she wore was tantamount to buying her a South Beach Diet cookbook or shipping her off to fat camp. I mean, I don't have major self-esteem issues or anything like that, but who wanted to be talking body type with a hottie of the opposite sex?

Well, at least talking about clothing sizes was the exact opposite of blatantly flirting.

"I wear a medium," I offered as a vague but appropriate response to a loaded question.

"Hmm."

Oh, jeez, did he not believe me? Did he think I was too skinny? Not skinny enough? Maybe he was thinking about my ankles. I've always suspected that my ankles are thick. In the summer I have a really hard time finding sandals that make my feet look delicate rather than like huge, puffy loaves of bread.

And *why,* oh why, was I being plagued with these thoughts? Obviously, my pledge to myself meant absolutely nothing. I couldn't even trust my own little inner voice. It was bad enough that I was so easily distracted that Seth sometimes had to tell me things three times in a row. It was bad enough that Seth had a chemical effect on me during our class on Saturdays. But now I was going to be constantly sidling past him by the pick-up window, past the break room, or at the computer at the end of the bar. With my big old bread-loaf feet. Seth was adorable, but that wasn't supposed to matter to me right now—I had more than enough going on without being distracted by the latest cute boy to cross my path.

He couldn't be a crush. And he couldn't be a boyfriend (the mere mention of the word gave me shivers—the bad kind of shivers, that is).

Well, then—we were just going to have to be coworkers. And coteachers. And cocookers.

The combo sounded bland, even inside my head.

"Well," Seth's voice cut into my mental monologue, reminding me yet again that focus was probably really important here at Hype. It was my job, I'd decided, to surreptitiously raise the caliber of the service at Hype. I could do that, at least, if nothing else. I mean, I was an overachiever. Kicking butt at whatever I tried my hand at was sort of second nature.

My phone call with my mother, when she had complained to me about her first visit to Hype, weighed on me like a sixteen-ounce package of potato gnocchi that'd been boiled, strained, and left in a bowl at room temperature for two hours too long. Mom had nothing good to say about Hype, which meant that sooner or later, unless the situation at Hype did a complete one-eighty, she'd be publishing a negative review.

My skin crawled just thinking about it. Even though Seth and I couldn't be involved romantically, a bad review from my mother probably wouldn't go over all that well. *Especially* since I still hadn't told him what my mom does for a living. *And* we still had to teach together at the rec center. Meanwhile, Mom would freak when I told her that I was working at Hype. Not because I took on an extra job. (Well, probably not—although she was one of those people who were of the belief that I tended to spread myself too thin. She always said I was sixteen going on forty-six). No, she'd freak because it was weird for me to keep this job from her. Just like it was weird to hide my mom's job from Seth.

Oh, boy. I was in over my head. This was all going to come back to bite me in the butt, right?

"Laine?" Seth snapped his fingers in front of my face.

Whoops.

"Training. Check." I mock-saluted him, which, thankfully, made him smile.

"Just for today, you'll be shadowing someone," he explained. "It should give you a feel for how the shift tends to break down."

I nodded. "Cool." I wanted—and desperately didn't want—to shadow Seth. I had a feeling that would involve creating all sorts of kooky reasons to knock into him or otherwise initiate physical contact.

He patted me on the shoulder, and I allowed my fantasy to take off. Maybe we'd even get married here at Hype one day.

This line of thinking was so the opposite of my personal anticrush oath. Grr.

Seven

"Callie."

I realized I'd been standing with my eyes closed. I blinked them wide open again. My name wasn't Callie. Seth knew my name. Didn't he?

"Hey, Seth."

Oh.

That was another voice. Another voice entirely. Another *female* voice, to be precise. And it belonged to a female person.

Ugh.

It was a good thing I didn't have romantic designs on Seth, because I got the feeling that if I had actively pursued him, Callie might have had a thing or two to say about it. She clearly hated me, and more than that, she was used to getting her own way. I could tell both of these things simply by looking at her: Her lush, caramel-colored waves were the waves of a girl for whom things were done. No one with hair like that ever had to prove herself to someone else.

I disliked her. Intensely.

It seemed that the feeling was mutual.

"Hi." She practically hissed at me. Callie squinted her hazel eyes at me suspiciously.

I wanted to tell her to chill out. She didn't need to worry about me. I'm no circus freak, but, as I've mentioned, I'm quirky whereas she is more modelesque. So it wasn't like I was going to bump her out of the running for the "Miss Hype" competition running through my mind. And besides, I was Not. Crushing. This. Summer. Period. And you can't compete with someone who's forfeited the game, right?

"I guess I'll be mentoring you, Lynn," Callie said, smirking and shaking my hand with her own French-manicured fingers.

"Actually, it's——," I started.

"Awesome!" Callie said, cutting me off. "Seth wants you to shadow me today." She spat out the word "shadow" like it was more along the lines of "poison with arsenic."

"I'm just going to give her an intro to prep work," she said, speaking directly to Seth. I couldn't help but notice the shift in her demeanor when she looked at him instead of me. "Once she's changed. You are changing, right?"

She turned back toward me, scowling again. "I think the last waitress left her uniform behind. She's bigger than I am, so her uniform should fit you just fine."

I could smell an insult when it was dropped into thin air. This girl, who until five minutes ago I did not even know existed, seemed to hate me with the heat of a thousand fiery suns—for reasons that were not entirely clear.

For now I forced myself to mentally calculate how much tip money I'd need in order to make it through one semester at college. The sum I came up with was in the vague neighborhood of "a lot." I decided to let Callie's attitude go. It wasn't worth jeopardizing my job performance.

As I shimmied awkwardly past the bar and toward the unisex bathroom that the restaurant employees used, I felt a hand pat me on the back. I wheeled around and found myself face to face with Damien. "Don't mind Callie," he stage-whispered to me. "You're going to be fine."

Was he flirting? Or just being friendly? I was pretty sure he was flirting (radar, remember?). Either way, his eyes were a hypnotic shade of green, and I totally appreciated the small gesture of kindness. Old habits, right? I'd probably be a fickle little flirt until my dying day, wheeling myself around the nursing home winking crookedly at the eligible bachelors in the joint.

"Thanks," I said, smiling. There was no harm in smiling at a cute boy, was there? Even if that meant my boy-o-meter was now buzzing in two different directions?

"Don't mention it." When he grinned, his cheeks dimpled. It was totally adorable. "If you have any questions, just come and find me. I work most nights because I've got college loans to pay."

I did the mental math. He was a bartender. That meant he was at least twenty-one—too old for me. But I couldn't help it if I was attracted to him, could I? Dude radiated hotness in every direction. He was like a tornado of heat.

I tried to convince myself that it was

actually a good thing that Damien was so attractive. If nothing else, it would keep me from fixating on Seth. In that way it was sort of a distraction from my current distraction.

I was starting to confuse even myself. I pursed my lips and tried to look pensive and mature, like someone who worked to pay off college loans, rather than someone who was in high school but obsessively planning out her college budget about a hundred years in advance. I knew from hot guys, and they did not, as a general rule, find good organizational skills to be a turn-on. (If they did, I would be so unstoppable.)

"Let me know if Callie gets to be too much for you. She's not exactly a girl's girl, but I've got your back." He winked.

OMG. Seth may have been adorable, but Damien exuded dangerous hotness, like that drugged-out guy on *Heroes*. (Which was not to say that I thought Damien did drugs. At least, I hoped he didn't.) He could *totally* get my back, if he wanted.

If you can't stand the heat, get out of the kitchen. That's how the saying goes, right? Damien was hot. Seth was hot. Heck, Callie wasn't exactly my type, but I had to admit that even she was hot. Hype was practically a hothouse.

I felt invigorated. I knew waiting tables would be work, and I knew the work would be hard. I wasn't trying to kid myself about that. But as far as the work environment went, I was, for the moment, a happy little hothouse flower.

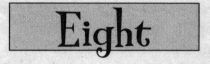

Eight

"Uh, Laine?"

It was Pete, tugging insistently at my sleeve and looking concerned but decidedly nonchalant, all at once.

I smiled at him affectionately, despite the fact that any moment now, I was sure to let out my best primal scream.

It was the Fourth of July, and while Anna was enjoying red white and blue ice pops courtesy of the Cabana Club caterers, I was stuck working a booth at the Halliday Fantastic Fourth celebration. I loved my students. Really, I did. And I was proud of the blizzard of desserts we had whipped up the previous Saturday, in a maniacal burst of collective energy.

But seriously?

I was tired.

No, it was more than that. I was, like, completely and totally overcooked. My pilot light was fast flickering out. Between shifts at Hype and teaching the cooking course, I was rapidly running out of steam.

But that wasn't Pete's fault.

"Yes?" I asked him, sneaking a handful of the gummy bears we had set up in a give-away bowl and stuffing them into my mouth. My cheeks puffed out like a strung-out squirrel's. Very professional.

"Are there, um, preservatives in the apricot cobbler?"

I drummed my fingers against the table-top. "Who wants to know?"

He squinted and pointed somewhat conspicuously to a bleached-blond soccer mom who looked Botoxed and yogafied within an inch of her (undoubtedly extremely health-ful) life.

"Did you tell her that we use apricot *preserves* in the apricot cobbler?" I asked, taking care to speak slowly and reign in at least 60 percent of my frustration. "Preserves that may be fortified with preservatives."

He nodded. "Yeah. She wanted me to

double-check, you know, whether or not we used only organic ingredients."

Right.

I wished. As much as Seth and I made a point of emphasizing healthy living, we did not have the budget to shop at the local food co-op, where a loaf of organic bread cost a bazillion and five dollars. Personally, I would have preferred to use some less processed, more exotic ingredients. But the whole point of the class, I guess, was to relate to the kids on their own level. Or so Nora kept telling me whenever I came to her with an idea for jazzing up a classic recipe.

I waved my hand at him in a "not so much" sort of gesture. He smiled and ambled off to break the news to Fit Mom.

I felt a tap on my shoulder. I turned to find Barrie, looking distraught. Her bright red hair was pulled into two taut pigtails, which added a surreal touch to her anxiety. In culinary parlance, she looked not unlike a certain red-headed spokesperson for a well-known fast-food joint. Although, at the moment, she was considerably less chipper than that other, trademarked, animated floating redhead.

"We have a problem," she said gravely.

Seeing as how she was clearly not hurt or otherwise in distress, I bit the insides of my cheeks and struggled not to giggle. I mean, someone with as many freckles as Barrie just cannot get away with grave anxiety. It simply doesn't work.

"Oh?" I raised a single eyebrow—a trick that the students found endlessly fascinating. It's the little things, really.

"It's Gretchen," Barrie offered, still pretty much breathless. "She says the chocolate chocolate chip cookies are undercooked."

This scenario was entirely plausible. Our kitchen equipment wasn't totally reliable, and, as I may have mentioned, a bunch of twelve-year-olds aren't the most patient people you'll find. Not that I was all that much better about the self-discipline. I still had a little burn on the roof of my mouth from some overzealous and premature tasting of a batch of éclairs last week.

I had to think fast. "Some people like their cookies undercooked," I reminded Barrie, serious as an untouched packet of Splenda. "There's a whole cottage industry of packaged raw cookie dough that's sweeping the nation."

Barrie rolled her eyes. Obviously, I was being a very moronic older-type person.

"Duh," she said. "It's just that she's worried. Because *some* people"—she said this part very self-righteously and allowed herself a furtive glance to each side before continuing—"think the situation could be dangerous."

I scrunched my forehead up in total confusion. To the best of my knowledge, there were very few scenarios in which a cookie could be called "dangerous," undercooked or not. I seriously think that salmonella hoo-ha is at least 74 percent hysterical parenting.

"I think we'll be fine," I said, trying not to sound patronizing. "Cookies aren't really—"

I was unceremoniously cut off by an enormous gob of chocolate chocolate chip cookie dough that hit me squarely in the chest, bouncing off of my nonboobs and leaving an unattractive stain right in the middle of my favorite baby blue long-sleeve baseball T-shirt.

Oh, that was so totally not coming out in the wash.

"That's the thing," Barrie said. She may or may not have sounded slightly smug.

"Right, okay," I said, clapping her on the shoulder briskly. "Why don't you duck and cover, and I'll, ah . . . have a word with everyone about what is and is not considered appropriate Fantastic Fourth behavior."

Before Barrie had a chance to trot off, there was deep belly laughter from behind me, and I knew it could mean only one thing: Seth had been witness to my humiliation.

Sure enough, when I whirled around, I found him wiping at the corners of his eyes. He was lucky. Only a boy as cute as he was could get away with taking so much pleasure in my pain.

Not that I was noticing his cuteness, or boy-type people in general, this summer.

Nope. Not I. Not at all.

"You're laughing at me," I said.

He swallowed a particularly enthusiastic guffaw and, to his credit, managed to straighten up for a nanosecond before collapsing back into hysterics again.

"I am," he managed to squeak, once he'd regained a tiny sliver of his composure. "Sorry." He shook his head and wiped at his eyes again.

"You're laughing so hard you're *crying*,"

I said, lowering my voice to a totally non-threatening growl.

"I can't help it," he said, practically gasping the words out.

He took a deep breath and somehow managed to get it together. "I'll make it up to you," he swore.

"How?" I was suspicious. I kind of liked the idea of Seth being indebted to me, but it had to be too good to be true. It for sure was a violation of the no-flirting policy that dictated my entire summer social life.

"You go clean up," he said, gesturing to my now semisweet T-shirt. "I'll pay a visit to the frontlines, take care of the warring camps."

Barrie scowled. "Why do I think this means you won't let any of us retaliate?"

I chuckled. "She has a point, Seth," I reminded him. "After all, revenge is sweet."

I was scrubbing vigorously at the front of my shirt when Seth tracked me down outside the girls' bathroom. Adding to the humiliation of being pelted with raw cookie dough was the need to wash it off in a public restroom. This shirt was *so* going to need to be replaced. Grr.

Seth peered at me cautiously, probably because I radiated intense grouchy rays in all directions.

"Stain Stick?" he offered tentatively.

I smiled. "Definitely. But even then we've only got a 50 percent chance of recovery." I thought for a moment. "What are you doing with a Stain Stick, anyway? You don't strike me as the kind of person to carry a laundry basket in his pockets."

Seth laughed, showing his even, white teeth. Seriously, he totally looked like an "after" picture for those teeth-bleaching solutions.

"I'm full of surprises," he said simply.

Oh, man. If that was true, then I was in even more trouble than I thought. Stain Stick kinds of surprises were actually the way to my heart.

"You thought it was safe to leave them alone?" I asked, meaning, of course, our miniarmy of Rachael Ray juniors. (Yes, I was changing the subject. Surprisey Seth was starting to make me blush, and I needed to get myself back together.)

"Well, I put Gretchen in charge," he replied. It kind of made sense. She seemed pretty earnestly opposed to food fights, which made her unique among a good chunk of her peers.

"So, which is harder?" Seth ventured, as I tossed the last of the soggy used paper towels into a trash can. "Teaching the class or waiting tables at Hype?"

Even with a gajillion-ton ball of cookie dough having come at me at light speed, this was a no-brainer.

"Hype." My eyes widened, conveying the trauma and stress associated with that place. "Definitely Hype."

He laughed at my wild-eyed expression.

I was *so into* it when Seth laughed. Even if it was at me.

We were definitely verging into flirting territory.

"It's not that bad," he insisted.

"It's not *that* bad," I agreed. "But it seems like I'm maybe not the most ideal candidate for a job that requires attention to detail. I get so . . . distracted."

"Well, the cooking class is hard core and you deal with that, right?" he asked.

"I have a partner for cooking class," I reminded him, "who keeps me on track." He grinned again, and his brown eyes twinkled. The power of those twinkly eyes was not to be underestimated. His gaze was steady, and suddenly I felt a little bit self-conscious.

Was this a Moment between us? Were we having a Moment? Because a Moment *definitely* counted as flirting.

"I mess things up at the restaurant," I said. Anything to break up the awkward, intense, thunderous silence. Surely I didn't have to actually remind him of the surfin' safari I took last Tuesday on a stray hunk of avocado? Surely he could recall that master stroke without prodding.

It was so frustrating. All my life, things had worked out for me: grades, friends, flings. Sure, I had to work at them, but when I worked, things worked out. I had blindly assumed that Hype would be the same.

I assumed wrong.

"And then there's my archnemesis," I continued. I didn't want to trash-talk Callie to Seth, because I thought it would make me sound petty. But it was what it was. She detested me, inexplicably, and was constantly going out of her way to give me a hard time. Her latest shtick was forcing me to "marry" all of the ketchup bottles—

midshift, when there was no way to balance side work with turning tables.

Brat.

"Don't let her get to you," Seth said. "I'm sure she's just jealous."

I snorted. "Jealous of *me*? Doubtful." I stepped back and regarded Seth again curiously. "But, I mean, if she *were* jealous of me . . . why would that be?"

Suddenly a flush erupted over Seth's face, creeping up from his neck until the tips of his ears were blazing.

This was an unexpected reaction.

"There could be a reason," he mumbled, looking like he kind of wanted the floor to open up and whisk him away to an alternate reality where no one ever has to live through embarrassing situations.

I shook my head. More and more it was looking like we were having a real, live *Moment*, which was—well, let's face it— pretty much the cherry on the ice cream sundae of my life. Like, maybe it was going to melt, so I should just eat it all up while I could.

I was rationalizing my crush. Was this one of the five stages of denial?

The tension in the air threatened to turn

me (and, I thought, Seth, too) inside out. I had to break it up.

"We should go see how Gretchen's doing and what's going on over there," I suggested.

Seth nodded enthusiastically, and I could see relief flood his extra-adorable features.

I waved in the general direction of our booth.

And then I realized what, exactly, was going on over there.

And I froze.

Nine

Okay, so maybe I was being a little bit melodramatic—but only a *little* bit, I swear. The thing was, when I turned back to our stand, I saw not only Gretchen, Pete, and the rest of our precocious cooking disciples, but also the very last person I wanted to run into at the Fantastic Fourth celebration.

Yeah, it was my mother.

Now, under normal circumstances, I would have no problem running into my mother at an event like this. My mom, more than anyone except maybe Anna, is one of my very biggest supporters. So normally it would be great for her to see me here with the students—them looking studious (or as studious as one can look with chocolate chips mashed into one's hair) and me looking teacherly.

Under *normal* circumstances, that is.

Despite the fact that, between Hype and the cooking class, Seth and I were spending a bunch of days a week together, I had somehow managed to keep from telling him about what my mom does for a living. I knew, based on a few years of personal experience, that when a foodie finds out your mother is a big-time restaurant critic, well, everyone gets kind of antsy. And knowing what my mom thought about Hype—at least, for now—clearly the best course of action would be to try like holy heck to keep Seth and Mom from ever meeting up.

This was going to be a problem.

Snapping back from my internal panic attack, I saw Seth walk toward the bake sale and periodically glance backward to see if I was following.

These were desperate times, my friends.

"Wait!" I called in a tone of voice more suitable for a small grease fire or a set of diners skipping out on their four-figure restaurant check.

Seth halted in place, looking appropriately concerned.

He really was *so* sweet.

Right, he wanted to know what had me so hyped up.

Think fast, Laine.

"Um, I think that Pete is a mess from the food fight."

It was a safe bet. I mean, Pete had been standing not three feet away from the fray. I pointed at my chest, just in case Seth didn't remember from five seconds ago. "I'll send him to you for a good hose-down."

Seth looked appropriately bewildered, so I took the opportunity to jog over to our table.

I was concentrating so fiercely on keeping one eye on Seth that I stumbled directly into my own mother.

"Unnecessary roughness," she called, grabbing at my shoulders and lightly wrestling me out of her personal space. Once she'd created a few inches of distance between us, she looked me over.

"Laine, did you know that the chocolate chocolate chip—"

"Undercooked. Yeah, we've been over that." I *needed* to send Pete over to Seth before Seth came back to the table. This was dire. The process would be as delicate as baking a soufflé.

"Pete," I hissed, sidling over to him and nudging him in the ribs, "were you having a food fight with Cameron before?"

He looked at me with wide eyes. The expression on his face clearly showed a lack of any involvement in airborne cookie dough. But something about my desperation must have shown on *my* face.

Bless his little caramel-coated heart, he nodded

"Go get cleaned up," I suggested. "Seth is looking for you." This was not, strictly speaking, true. But it worked. Pete cast a last baleful glance at me and wandered warily toward the public bathrooms.

I was safe—for the next few minutes, at least.

I turned back to my mother.

"Some people like the cookies under-cooked," I said, crossing my arms over my chest defensively.

My mother laughed. "Fair enough," she agreed. "Anyway, I didn't come over here to pick on you. I just wanted to see what you and your class have been up to."

I spread my arms wide. "Behold a bounty of baked goods. Try the cobbler. Loaded with preserved goodness."

Sure, behold. But then please go away so you don't out me.

She started fiddling with the clasp on her bag. "Give me two of whatever you think I'll like best."

Seth was going to come back any minute. I could *not* be dealing with change right now. I'm just not good with numbers. It wouldn't be a pretty—or speedy—process.

"You know what," I stammered, shooing her away with my hands, "we're all going to be taking the leftovers home, so, you know, your money's no good here."

She wrinkled her forehead. "I just wanted to support—"

"Yeah, of course, that's totally sweet," I said, speaking in a massive rush.

Ah! *There* was my flash of inspiration.

"It's just that the *Sun* has a table over there"—I jerked my head due west—"and they're selling ad space. A *lot* of it," I added ominously.

The *Sun* is the *Tribune*'s top competitor. They were sponsoring a writing program for teens this summer, and they'd gotten a lot of publicity for it. My mom was sick of hearing about it, so I could count on her to have a reaction to this new information.

Her eyebrows flew upward in perfect arches. "I see." She drummed her fingers on the table thoughtfully, then shrugged. "All right. If you would rather bring home leftovers, it's up to you. Maybe I'll go check out the *Sun*'s table."

Right, maybe.

I nodded, my face impassive. "Good plan." I clapped her on the back and smiled broadly. "See you later!"

She looked at me strangely for a beat or two, but she took the bait.

I only hoped that there actually was a *Sun* booth at this street fair.

Oh, well. Dwelling on that wouldn't help me now.

I was safe, at least for a little while.

Sweet.

Ten

It was almost too good to be true. My too-hot-to-handle scenario had been temporarily tamped down by two tiny little white lies. Mom didn't know about Seth, and Seth didn't know about Mom. I had one juicy secret, that was for sure. And I was going to keep it all to myself for as long as I possibly could.

Unfortunately, I didn't really know how long that would be. Ever since my Moment with Seth on the Fourth of July, I'd been fantasizing that "us," as a couple, was possible. Suddenly it seemed not-insane to think that he could find me as yummy as I found him. I mean, he'd blushed and all. At the Fantastic Fourth, he'd blushed. In boy-speak, blushing means something, right?

And what about the fact that I was now fully *obsessing* about his facial pigmentation? Did that mean that I had progressed from crush to full-blown, sizzling feelings? Feelings were new. Feelings were complicated. Feelings were *scary*.

So I decided to try not to have them.

All of my sweet-as-pie feelings about Seth were making it harder than ever to concentrate at Hype. And yet . . .

The situation was starting to feel as sticky as an all-day sucker.

My preoccupation was not a good thing. Really—just ask the irate elderly couple sitting over at table nineteen. The ones who asked for their water, like, a year ago.

"Hel-*lo*."

It actually wasn't Mr. and Mrs. Grumpy, but rather Callie, on her way to the computer to type in an order. She was kind enough to accidentally-on-purpose slam her hip into me on her way.

I shook my head, startled. Her hips were narrower than an eleven-year-old boy's, and she still couldn't see fit not to trample all over me? People who are genetically blessed really ought to be kinder toward those of us less gifted.

"Sorry. I spaced." It was half true; I *had* spaced. But I wasn't all that sorry. Maybe I should have been, but Callie was a grade-A, prime beyotch. Not only that, but she was the worst kind of beyotch—one who was startlingly attractive. Grr.

"Really?" Her voice dripped with sarcasm.

I resisted the intense urge to throttle her. It was most definitely illegal and probably wouldn't reflect well on me to Seth, or his dad, either. Even if, technically, I would only be force-feeding Callie her just deserts.

"Laine." She was crankier now. Much crankier. It was kind of weird; most human beings, like, max out at a certain level of crankiness, but not Callie. Callie had bitchery in reserves.

"Yeah?" I willed myself to go to my Zen place. I was in a land where chunky peanut butter and milk chocolate merged in a beautiful symphony of creamy, sugary goodness. . . .

Shoot. Now I was drifting off again.

I stood up straight and blew my bangs up and off my forehead. "Yeah."

Callie grimaced at me. "Table nineteen."

"Right, the water." I moved to take care

of it. I couldn't believe I'd gotten distracted *again*.

See? Love: not worth the trouble. It *always* gets in the way. And if, as I suspected, my feelings for Seth ran deeper than a simple crush, you could just triple that trouble. And then double it again.

"*Not* the water," Callie interjected. "Although they'd probably be into that, too." She rolled her eyes so hard I wondered if she could see the inside of her perfectly shaped skull. "I *think* they're ready to order."

Whoops. My bad. Even I knew that "think" was code for "know for a fact," with a hint of "you dingbat" thrown in.

"Right," I assured her. "I'll take care of it."

As the night went on, I did my best to tend to table nineteen as well as the four others that were located in my station. It's just, waiting tables was so overwhelming and difficult, and it was exactly the sort of task that my left-brain-oriented self wasn't really suited for. Even if Callie hadn't been launching a one-woman campaign against me, I still would have been in the weeds, big-time.

Why did I do this to myself? If I was such a lousy waitress, why didn't I quit?

The simple truth? I needed the money.

The more difficult truth? The one I wasn't sure I was ready to face yet? I *really* wanted Seth.

Since the Fourth of July, an electric force field had bubbled up between Seth and me. It had gotten to where I could barely stand to look directly at him without sunglasses or a hazmat suit or . . . I don't know. *Something.*

But you know who else stuck to Seth like a half-melted Tootsie Roll? Callie. What this meant was that I was not only avoiding Callie, but I was doing my best to duck and cover whenever Seth was around too.

This obviously involved a lot of leaping through doorways and slinking down hallways when either of them swung by. If nothing else, I was getting a good workout.

I was so busy both stressing out and bussing table seventeen that at first I didn't notice Anna walk into the restaurant. Once she caught my eye, though, I let out a squeal of glee, quickly stashed my tray at the sideboard in front of the kitchen, and dashed over to her. It was bliss to see a familiar face in the place I now thought of as a heretofore undiscovered tenth circle of hell.

"*What* are you doing here?" I asked, totally shocked.

"The kiddie has pinkeye and is deathly contagious. So I get a few days off." She winked at me with a decidedly non-pink eye.

"Lucky," I pouted.

"Uh, I'm not the one who's working with Mr. Crest Whitestrips, Laine," she pointed out.

There was that, yeah. She'd come by and seen Seth before, and, like anyone with eyes, realized that he was smokin' hot.

I grinned. "Thank goodness for that. I would hate to have to kill you."

"So . . . ," she hedged, "how *is* the competition these days?"

I bit my lip. Anna had decided over late-night café mochas with me that the source of Callie's hatred was jealousy. I tried to convince her that Callie had not one single reason to be jealous of me, but Anna wasn't buying. She thought that my not-crush on Seth was both not-nonexistent and not-nonobvious.

I held my right hand over my heart. "I plead the fifth, your honor."

"You're no fun," Anna groaned.

"I'm *so* fun," I corrected her. I glanced at my watch. "And you know what's even more fun? You camping out at the bar with my good friend Damien"—I jerked my thumb in his direction—"while I finish up my shift."

"*Laine*, how long is that going to take? Be honest—I will totally kill you if you make me miss *The Daily Show*."

I shrugged. "That's why God invented TiVo," I reminded her. There wasn't time to snag her some of the "family dinner" that the staff was served before each shift, but I could poke my head into the kitchen and get her an order of steamed edamame to snack on.

"Now, get comfy," I told her as I ran off. "I'll be back with some food in a minute. Then I'll finish out my shift. And, in the meantime, Damien will take good care of you."

If there *was* a God, he or she was totally trying to mess with me, big-time. Hype was serving two specials that night, penne with sweet Italian sausage and rigatoni with spicy sausage.

I mean, you can see where I'd get confused, right? Two tubey little pastas? Two types of cured meat? When I made pasta, it was usually vegetarian. It almost seemed like a practical joke that Callie would pull.

Not even. A practical joke from Callie would probably have been easier to deal with than this. About every other order I brought out was wrong. In addition to annoying my customers, it aggravated the kitchen staff and stressed me out.

In truth, the amount of time I worked and Anna sat at the bar was something like an hour and a half. But running back and forth sweaty and disheveled, trying desperately not to let Seth catch me doing an all-around lousy job, was so exhausting it may as well have been a day and a half.

I was too worn out even to take it personally when I was the first waitress cut for the evening. For Anna, it was practically a cause for celebration, despite the fact that Damien had been making pleasant chit chat while I worked.

"Thank *God*," she groaned dramatically as we grabbed our bags on and made our way outside.

"For small favors?" I couldn't help but

add my own two cents. Because really, this had been one teeny-tiny favor. The blisters on my feet screamed with every step. And like I said, it wasn't really such a good thing being the first person sent home at the end of the night. It certainly didn't say much good stuff about my job performance.

"Whatever, Laine. You're lucky that we got you out of there when we did." Anna rolled her eyes at me and dug into her bag for some lip balm, which she proceeded to apply liberally. When she was done, she offered the tube to me.

I shook my head. My lips were totally ragged from constant stressed-out biting. There was no saving them with drugstore solutions. "Was it really that obvious?"

She nodded vigorously. "Oh yes."

My stomach bottomed out. Anna was right. Seth's father was totally going to fire me. He was so busy at the restaurant that we still hadn't been properly introduced, but I didn't think that would prevent him from oh, say, firing me.

Oh, jeez. My not-boyfriend's father was totally going to kick my butt. I'd lose my job and my not-boyfriend all at the same time.

Of course, that *would* solve the problem of having to explain to Seth what my mother did for a living.

No. I didn't care. Getting fired was still too terrible to even contemplate. It was like when I learned that fat-free cheese was actually worse for you than eating smaller portions of the regular stuff. Devastating.

Anna coughed and went on. "I'm very sorry to tell you, but that girl Callie totally has it in for you. If I were you, I'd start sleeping with one eye open."

I marveled for a moment that she could be so cavalier if, in fact, the life of her best friend was truly in danger. But after that moment had passed I realized that the two of us were talking about totally separate catastrophes.

And how, even, had I found myself in the middle of two totally separate catastrophes? My alpha-personality had finally bottomed out. I was a robot set to malfunction. I'd been running off in too many different directions. Different *catastrophic* directions. I was a catastrophe magnet. I hadn't even done any SAT prep since before the Fantastic Fourth. I was now, officially, a slacker. It was a new experience for me. I didn't much care for it, to be honest.

I took a deep breath. It was time to spill my guts to my best friend.

"I'm kind of a mess," I said.

Anna snorted. "Well, yeah. *That's* sort of obvious."

Awesome. Good to know. Ouch. "Right. That's me. Messy."

Anna stopped in front of the bus stop. At this hour we probably had at least a short wait. By now I was beyond fading—I was wilting. It didn't help that it was five thousand degrees outside and about a bazillion percent humidity. My hair was flipping out at the ends insanely.

Even my *hair* was spazzy these days. I didn't know who Seth dated—or even if or when he dated—but I'm willing to bet that his date would have perfect, stick-straight tresses. The straight-tressed girls were the ones who usually got the guy in the end.

It was a good thing I had sworn off flirting this summer.

"*I* was referring to your archnemesis, Callie, and her plans for world domination," Anna clarified.

I swallowed nervously. "Isn't 'arch-nemesis' a little bit extreme?" (It wasn't. I knew that. I was just going for a healthy dose of denial.)

"Oh, I don't think so. She hates your guts," Anna continued cheerfully. "I wasn't kidding about you watching your back. She looks like the type to start a chick fight. I bet she's a hair puller."

"You're probably right," I agreed glumly. "But seriously? I have no idea why she's so pissy. I would say that she just got frustrated having me shadow her, but she kind of despised me even before that—like, from the moment she first saw me. And, I mean, it's not like we're in competition or anything."

If we were in competition? Callie would win. Keep in mind: caramel-colored hair. This is something that people—restaurant customers, managers, and other random, boy-type people—respond to.

"Maybe *you're* not competing with her, but let me tell you, she's definitely competing with you," Anna said, pressing her lips together knowingly.

"*Why?*" I sputtered. "That's insane." Like my hair. Exhibit A: spazzy hair?

"No," Anna corrected me shortly. "What's insane is that she and Damien dated for, like five minutes back in May and she's gone completely *Swimfan* on him since then. According to him, they didn't click. But I guess that's not the way she saw it."

I went through the pop-culture catalog in my brain. *Swimfan* equaled a blond chick becoming totally obsessed with a guy on her high school swim team. They made out in a pool and then she started stalking him.

Unfortunately, when practiced by an attractive teen of the female persuasion, stalking could be kind of hot to a guy. Which meant that I *really* needed to stay out of Callie's way.

Man, Anna was good. She could get the dirt on anyone or anything. I think it was her even composure; unlike me, she was chatty, warm, and huggy. It comforted people, prompted them to let their guard down. She should have been working for the tabloids.

"I like good gossip as much as the next romantically starved teenager," I said, "but I'm still not sure how any of this connects to me."

She stared at me like my hair had suddenly turned magenta. "You're kidding, right?"

I wasn't kidding. "If I were kidding, wouldn't I say something that's actually funny?" I pointed out.

She shook her head and clucked her tongue at me, as if suggesting I was just too simple to understand even the most basic of concepts. "Damien. Wants. You."

I tilted my head to the left and hopped up and down like I had water in my ear.

"I'm sorry, I think I heard you wrong," I said, after I'd righted myself again. "It sounded like you said that Damien wants me."

I was still getting the piercing, magenta-hair gaze.

"Yes," she confirmed, speaking slowly, like I was a six-year-old learning to spell. "And I'm pretty sure I'm speaking English. What's the what here?"

"You are," I assured her, my words coming out in a rush. "Speaking English, that is. It's just—Damien is a bartender."

Anna nodded.

"Which means he must be twenty-one."

Anna nodded again, not even blinking. It was fascinating, how stoic her face could be.

"Why would he like me?"

"Because in the history of people, twenty-one-year-old bartenders never have a crush on *slightly* younger girls?" Anna pointed out. "Especially cute ones who get adorably flustered at work?"

"We couldn't *really* date—I mean, we couldn't be serious," I protested, ignoring the backhanded compliment. "It's illegal."

Anna placed her right hand to her heart. "I swear to the god of reality TV that I won't make a citizen's arrest."

"You're funny."

(She wasn't being funny.)

I dug into my wallet for my bus pass as the bus came chugging down the street in a fit of exhaust fumes. It groaned to a halt in front of us and we boarded, settling ourselves up near the front. That huge, wide windshield was perfect for boy-watching.

"Anyway, I don't know why you're getting so freaked out. Damien's *hot*." Anna, the voice of logic.

"Well, duh." Of course Damien was hot; he was Milo Ventimiglia with blue eyes. Now that I think about it, I guess I have a thing for guys with dark hair, huh? I never realized I had a type. This summer job extravaganza was really teaching me a lot about myself. "I just assumed he was out of my league. There's that whole age difference thing, you know. And also, as I've mentioned, I'm *not dating* this summer. Boys are just a distraction."

"Um, yeah," Anna said. "That's the whole point."

I frowned, and she prodded me. "Say more."

"Like what?" I shrugged.

"Like how you like-like someone else, like more than a friend. Someone whose name rhymes with . . . peth?"

Damn, she was good. "How did you know?"

She stuck out her tongue. "Really?"

Yeah, she always could read me like a menu.

I sighed. "Seth's different," I protested. "He's not, you know . . . just another crush of the day."

Anna cackled. "No, he's the blue-plate special!"

"Well, he's special, all right," I admitted.

"Poor Laine," Anna said, clucking in mock sympathy. "One boy is lusting after her, and another just may be the guy of her dreams. It's a wonder Callie feels threatened by you."

I frowned. "Damien isn't *lusting* after me," I insisted, even though there was a tiny part of me that was easily flattered, and I sort of hoped that he was. "I just figured he was being friendly."

"You figured wrong," she said. "If this thing with Seth isn't happening—which, I don't mean to be rude, but how long have you guys been working together, and he hasn't asked you out?"

"Thanks for pointing that out," I interjected. "Very helpful. I *told* you, my flirt mode has been switched off."

"Since Seth hasn't asked you out," she continued doggedly, "I think you should consider going out with Damien. He's smart, cute, funny—and he makes a ton in tips every night. He told me so."

"Just like he told you that he was madly in love with me."

I knew Anna wouldn't make something like this up, but I was skeptical nonetheless. I could count on one hand how many times in my entire short life I'd been involved in a love triangle. Frankly, I could count it on *no* hands. Zero. Zero times. I didn't know from love triangles—I was a big fat love circle of zero times. I'd never dated a guy long enough for it to develop into any complicated geometric configurations.

So you could see where this news might come as a shocking—but exciting—surprise.

"Those weren't his exact words, but yeah, he's very into the Bettie Page hair—"

He liked my quirky hair? This was huge news. *Huge.* My sense of aesthetics was finally being validated, despite the disgusting humidity levels of late.

"—and I think, given his attraction, that he might be inclined to take you out for coffee. If you'd be into that."

I paused. *Would* I be into that?

"I don't know," I said slowly. "Remember the rule? No dating."

"Laine," Anna replied, "*I'm* not the one asking you out. Maybe you need to sleep on it. See how you feel by the time Damien gets around to posing the question. You never know. Besides, going out with someone once doesn't mean you're, like, a brazen hussy. It's just coffee." She took a deep breath. "It's not like not-dating has turned your whole world around."

She was right, of course, as much as I hated to admit it. You really do never know. And I didn't have to make up my mind just yet. Frankly, even knowing that some cool, older hottie thought I was cute was almost excitement enough. Especially knowing that he was being pursued by a slim-hipped goddess with caramel-colored hair. I can't lie: It was sort of really nice to think that Callie was actually jealous of me. And I was mildly relieved to know that she didn't totally despise me for no reason at all. I mean, she had sort of a reason, even if it was gross and petty. So call that the icing on the cake.

I was going to have to watch my back, though. Anna was right about that.

I guess you really *can't* have your cake and eat it too.

Eleven

Even if I wasn't convinced of my own babe-osity, Anna's words really stuck into my brain like so many stretchy strands of Laffy Taffy. Objectively speaking, it's not like I was physically deformed or anything, so it wasn't *completely* outside of the realm of possibility that she was right about Damien having, if not the full-blown hots, then at least the warms for me. Warms were not such a long shot.

The question was, did *I* have the warms for Damien? It was hard to say, probably because I just hadn't been thinking that way about him at all.

Anna was right; he was kind of the total package. He was hot, funny, smart, outgoing, and apparently made good money. (Thank goodness my best friend has no interest in boundaries. She asks the hard questions.) But there was also a reason I hadn't been thinking "that way" about him. A reason that had nothing to do with seasonal vows of chastity or the like.

A Seth reason.

True, nothing much had come of our overly hyped (no pun intended) Moment on the Fourth of July. Three weeks had passed, and I was starting to lose the glimmer of hope that that exchange had given me. Was it possible I'd hallucinated it? Was I a deranged Moment Magnifier?

Maybe. Maybe I was.

Even still, I wasn't completely ready to give up the squishy, chocolate-covered feelings I got whenever I was around Seth. Damien was like . . . like a Swedish fish. Completely yummy, and it would do in a pinch (I'm not one to turn down delicious gummy candy) . . . but somehow still less inspiring than a good hunk of Godiva. And I was kind of a Godiva girl.

I made a pact with myself: I'd give it one good, solid, honest-to-Godiva shot with Seth and see where that got me. Anna was right: I had real feelings for him. Forget flirtation—this could be a romance. I owed at least that much to myself before I abandoned all hope of a five-course relationship with my favorite cooking coconspirator.

I'd give it one shot with Seth, and if that didn't pan out, I'd head right back into the land of SAT prep, with no looking back.

On Saturday morning I awoke with the addled determination of a restaurant reviewer about thirty minutes before the weekend edition goes to press (for those of you not in "the biz": I was stressed).

I spent more time than usual choosing my wardrobe; it was imperative to dress comfortably and in clothing that could take a beating from a spray of assorted foodstuffs. But this week I had particular reason to want to look if not my very hottest, then at least my least quirky. In theory I had to channel my inner (nonbratty) Callie. I had to get my flirt back on. Assuming, of course, that I still had one.

In the end, I settled on a worn and comfortable pair of overalls over a bright long-sleeved T-shirt. Okay, so I'm quirky. I just am. I have to learn to love it. I wasn't going to show up at cooking class in peep-toed platforms and leggings. I just wasn't.

The bangs were behaving, and after thirty-seven minutes of deep concentration, I managed to work something out with my makeup where I looked completely fresh-faced and natural. Which I thought was kind of crucial in bringing what little inner Callie I did have to the surface. Inner Callie seemed like the type of girl who'd be well glossed, but subtly so.

Was it weird that my personal flirt mechanism seemed to be single-white-femaling my archnemesis? I didn't have time to give the matter further thought.

I stepped back to assess myself in the full-length mirror that stood in the corner of my bedroom. It was true: I would probably always be cute rather than hot, but I allowed myself the slight possibility that in this case, cute would be more than enough.

Feast your eyes, Seth.

And Callie, eat your heart out.

Yeah, as far as pep talks went, even I wasn't exactly buying it.

Oh, man. When it came to matters of

the heart, these days I was completely and totally out to lunch.

But hopefully not for long.

"Gentle with the dough, guys!"

Even to my own ears, my voice was scaling notes best reserved for dogs and superheroes. It made me cringe, but I couldn't help it. Dough was flying to and fro, and it was really just a matter of time before we were reenacting a slapstick scene from an old sitcom.

Why had Seth and I decided on pizza for our next class? Yes, pizza made from fresh dough.

Oh, yeah. Because Pete wasn't the only one with an Italian food fetish. Find me a kid who doesn't like pizza, and I'll find you a kid who's never tried it.

And as it turned out, making pizza was almost as much fun as eating it. For safety's sake, Seth and I had cordoned off the ovens, which were set to a level somewhere between "blistering" and "total meltdown." But we'd given everyone his or her own prep work, and they were happily prepping away—some more enthusiastically than others, hence my shrieking. Any minute now, Cameron, who kneaded away vigorously at a crust, was going to wind up wearing a pizza-dough bathrobe. While this would be amusing, it would also be a pain to clean up.

For my part, I was mixing together an industrial-sized tub of crushed tomatoes with a very precise blend of Italian herbs, which included an unexpected pinch of crushed red pepper, a secret ingredient passed down from my mom's mom's mom. There was lots of fine-chopping going on, which really wasn't my strong suit. I would much rather have pulverized a clove or two of garlic, tossed it in, and have been done with it (and I think the boys in our class would be way into the pulverization process as well). But, you know, Seth was all into lists and ingredients and recipes. Talk about left brain. If there was one area in my life in which I wasn't a complete control freak, it was in the kitchen. The kitchen is where you're supposed to play around a little bit.

Okay. I have to confess: There was a method to my culinary madness today. There was a reason that I was mincing Spanish onions with the precision of a brain surgeon. Today I was the saucer and Seth was officially in charge of the dough, so sooner or later we'd have to combine our efforts. As I pounded away at my bowl of tomato pulp, I inched closer and closer to Seth. I was curious to see how long it would take him to notice that his personal space was being invaded. Unfortunately, up until now, most of our respective attention had been spent on reining in Cameron, who, it seemed, was actively trying to stretch his hunk of dough out to as wide a diameter as possible. I was a little worried about him.

But not so worried that I couldn't also keep my eyes on the prize. I coughed conspicuously and slid my bowl a few centimeters closer to Seth.

"Looking good, Laine," he commented.

I froze. Success! The hour and a half that I put into my casual, kicky look for the day had *totally* paid off! I couldn't wait to tell Anna the news. She definitely thought it was time to give up on Seth.

"Thanks," I said offhandedly, trying to swallow the smile that twitched at the corners of my mouth. I ran my fingers through my hair, trying to be flirty. Unfortunately, this resulted in my depositing a glob of tomato sauce in my hair.

Seth leaned forward with a napkin and dabbed at my head. I almost swooned from the intimacy. If he was willing to get up close and personal with my scalp, then he for sure thought I was looking good.

Awesome.

He crumpled up his paper towel and tossed it aside. "That's probably just about ready for the pies," he continued, jerking his head toward my big old bowl.

Right. The sauce. The *sauce* was looking good. Anna wouldn't care so much about that. And his proximity to my scalp was pure charity.

"Just about," I agreed.

I sighed. Maybe Seth was the type of guy who was more interested in cooking than couture. Maybe he liked perfectly portioned meals rather than perfectly proportioned girls. Maybe the way to Seth's heart really *was* through his stomach.

Or maybe he just didn't like me.

It would be just my luck to *finally* decide that some guy was worthy of more than just your standard three-date fling, only to have him Like Me as a Friend.

I had enough friends. All at once, I was ready for the real deal. A *boy*friend.

If I was lucky, he preferred hair saturated with the occasional smear of marinara to hair blow-dried within an inch of its life.

Maybe, just maybe, he was the perfect guy for a flowering foodie like me.

He slid his oven stone aside and whirled around.

"Cameron, the dough stays *on the table*!"

He must've thought the sauce crisis had passed, because he dashed swiftly over to prevent Cameron from draping his pizza dough across an unwitting Marci's stool.

I patted at my hair, which was feeling kind of sticky and would probably dry in a stiff little clump. *Maybe* Seth preferred a line cook to a leading lady. Maybe.

But it sure wasn't looking that way.

Me: He's so not into me.
Anna: Damien? Laine, we've been over this. He's completely into you.
Me: Not Damien. Seth.
Anna: Well, we kind of knew *that*. Right?
Me: Gee, thanks.

Anna: Uh-uh. You do not get to turn this into a pity party. You have a very adorable second-runner-up waiting in the wings. Or should I say, waiting by the break room?

Me: *(snorting)* Right, because there's nothing more romantic than semisweet nothings whispered across half-empty ketchup bottles.

Anna: Well, in that case, you'll have to let me know when you're ready to reel in your next catch of the day. The Cabana Club is teeming with gorgeous lifeguards, and I feel a new relationship coming on. I have my own fish to fry.

Me: By all means, fry away. I'll just be over here by the salad bar, wilting like week-old spinach.

Twelve

I had to face facts: Though the kitchen at cooking class had generated plenty of heat, none of it was of the romantic kind that I was dying for between Seth and me. And the longer we continued *not* heating things up, the more my sad little one-way crush was feeling like a plate of limp, warmed-over leftovers. I was turning into the human equivalent of a doggie bag, a concept I found thoroughly unappetizing.

I tried to throw myself back into my old patterns. I busted out my school yearbook and scanned the back pages to see which of the activities and clubs looked promising. I made new vocabulary flash cards. I subscribed to a *Naked Chef* podcast and cooked a new recipe for myself (and Mom, if she was home) every night.

It didn't work. I was still stuck on Seth. My tried-and-true techniques were starting to fail me. What would be next—my George Foreman grill shorting out?

On Saturday night I headed back to Hype. I knew Seth would be there. He'd mentioned to me that he was working a double shift, which meant he'd be properly zombified by the time I arrived, and maybe more susceptible to my many tasty charms. At least tonight—I hoped—I wouldn't get spaghetti sauce in my hair.

I arrived to find the dinner rush in full swing. Seth was nowhere to be seen, but Damien was at the bar, clearly slammed.

"Hey," I called to him as I made my way toward the back, where the break-room lockers were.

He beckoned to me. "Laine."

Dutifully, I backtracked to the bar. It didn't seem like it would be such great timing for a casual chat, so I was curious what he had to say.

He leaned over the polished wood. "Just a heads up. Boss man is here tonight, and he's breathing down our necks."

I gulped. Boss man was Seth's father. Seth's father whom I still hadn't met, who still didn't know that I was kind of a lousy waitress, and who had no idea I was kind of in hot-and-heavy like with his son. *And*, for some reason, every single person in Philadelphia who had ever idly wondered about upscale American cuisine had found their way to Hype tonight, at exactly the same time.

That was not going to be good.

Probably one of the few bright spots in a night like tonight was that even Callie was too harried to hit me with any of her usual vitriol. Her trademark hair was pulled tightly into two braids (adorable, of course) and her silver-lined eyes were bright and no-nonsense. She barely even glanced up as I rushed back out of the break room and hastily tied my apron at my waist.

"Table two wants breadsticks," she told me, actually managing not to spit at me for once.

"Right." I pivoted and turned sharply back in the direction from which I'd come, which was where we stashed things like salt, pepper, cutlery, and bread baskets.

Unfortunately, I wasn't the only one headed in that direction.

Before I could take even a full step forward, I collided into something thick and solid—like a tree trunk, but wearing a black polo shirt and pants. Seeing as most tree trunks do not wear polo shirts and khakis, and also aren't usually found inside casual-upscale urban eateries, this development was probably not good.

The collision was followed by a reverberant thud, and then the crash of many, many pieces hitting the floor.

This development was *so* not good.

My tree trunk? Was Seth. And he was covered in the detritus of at least three different entrées—the parts of them that weren't slowly leaking across the floor beneath us, that is.

My eyes flew open. More than anything, I wanted to be swallowed up into the giant dry-goods pantry, never to be seen or heard from again. Was that really not an option?

"Um, sorry," I squeaked, frozen in abject mortification.

"It's okay," Seth said generously, though his tight smile and stiff shoulders suggested otherwise. "It's pretty hectic here tonight."

"I should have looked where I was going," I gushed, crouching down to help him gather the fallout of our culinary collision.

"Don't worry about it," he said graciously.

It was beyond kind of Seth to be so pleasant about the fact that he was now wearing today's pasta special. At least it was a white sauce. That was something, given my track record with marinara. I could tell he was freaking out, though. His forehead was dotted with little beads of sweat, and his shoulders had crept up to his ears.

"Let me get this," I pleaded, stacking broken dinner plates onto my once-clean tray. "Seriously." Never mind that I hadn't even punched in yet, or checked in on any of my tables. I'd been here twenty minutes and I was already in the weeds.

No, not the weeds. Weeds would have been a delightful day trip. I was in the marshes, in quicksand, and I was going down fast.

"Uh, you know what would be really helpful?" Seth asked, glancing up, obviously hoping we weren't being too conspicuous.

As if. We were two people ankle-deep in overly hyped food. Not to mention that the crash had been in total surround sound. The only people who hadn't noticed us were people who weren't actually inside the restaurant at that moment.

"What? Sure. Anything," I said. It was way bad enough to suck at waitressing all by myself. But to cut into Seth's night? *Quel* humiliation.

He handed me a streaked and crumpled sheet of paper from his check pad. "Can you please just run these orders through the computer again? That way, the table won't have to wait forever for new food. I'll go explain what happened."

"Of course," I said, sounding desperate and breathless. "And, you know, after that I can totally help you clean the rest of this up—"

"No, no," he said. His voice was high-pitched and mildly frantic. He wanted me gone from the scene of the crime. That much was obvious. I was supremely embarrassed.

Oh, man. I was toxic. I was a toxic waitress.

Could a toxic waitress ever morph, butterfly-like, into a less-toxic girlfriend?

I shook my head. I was the last person to answer that question. And anyway, this was definitely not the time to be dwelling on my doomed love for Seth. The closest I'd get to his body—tonight, if not forever—was that kitchen crash test.

I darted off to punch his orders back in. The heat was really and truly on tonight, and I had to step up my game before things reached a boiling point.

It didn't take long to send Seth's orders through to the kitchen; I'm actually much better at a keyboard than a sideboard. I'd popped my head inside to explain what happened. No one was all that pleased with me, but they were too busy to do more than grunt disapprovingly while sautéing, mixing, and saucing mechanically (and maniacally).

I bumped into Callie—for once, not in the literal sense of the word, but actually merely brushed past her—on my way back to the front of the house (restaurant-speak for where the tables are). I braced myself for an onslaught of snark, but, still overwhelmed, she barely glanced at me.

"You've got a two-top. Just seated," she said, motioning toward table three. She made a face like she smelled sour milk. "Total freakshow."

Great. A weirdo. The last thing I needed tonight. Hadn't I already fulfilled my quota of embarrassment for the evening? For my life?

Seth's order was taken care of, and our mess had been cleaned (busboys: the true unsung heroes of the restaurant industry). Somewhere in the middle of all the chaos, I'd managed to get bread plates, water, and drink orders to my tables. It was finally time to tackle the wild card over at table three.

I quickly knotted my hair into a tiny ponytail and took a deep breath. Some meditation might have helped, but I doubted that this was the time to channel my inner Buddhist. I picked up my freshly wiped tray, exhaled, and at last turned toward table three.

And nearly fainted dead away.

Callie was right about the customer. Weird wasn't even the word. On the spectrum between "regular person" and "funhouse attraction," based on her appearance alone, she was inching swiftly and steadily away from the safety zone.

She sat unself-consciously by herself, thumbing idly through a magazine. I couldn't see from where I stood what she was reading, but I couldn't have missed her glasses in the dark: They were oversized pink plastic rims the likes of which Carrie Donovan only dreamed about. Her hair shot out from her face in a thick shock of bright copper curls. Her lipstick—a shade best described as "Bozo Red #1," extended well beyond her lip line, even though her mouth was closed, and it wouldn't have surprised me to learn that some had smudged onto her front teeth. She wore a green corduroy jumper that was about three sizes too big for her, and around her neck she'd strung a chain of oversized, multicolored plastic beads.

I knew this woman. Her name was Audrey.

And she was my mother.

Blindsided did not describe how I felt. When I realized that my mother was in the restaurant, in full review costume, it was as if the walls had shrunk inward to the point that they encased me, arms pinned at my sides. I couldn't move. I couldn't breathe. Time stood still, and everyone and everything in the room ground to a halt, like the gears had been soaked in pesto aioli and left out to rust.

I couldn't wait on my own mother. Not like this. She was a reviewer. A reviewer who already had plenty of her own ideas about this place. I certainly wasn't going to make it any better. And besides, wasn't there some law about this, like how doctors aren't supposed to operate on members of their own family?

But I *had* to wait on my mother. If I explained to anyone about the family clause, I'd blow her cover. That was out of the question, for sure.

I couldn't foist her table off on anyone else under flimsy, false pretenses, because there *wasn't* anyone else who wasn't buried. Swapping tables right now would only gum up the works further, and I wasn't exactly known for helping to keep Hype running in a smoothly (extra-virgin olive)-oiled fashion.

I had no choice. I had to step up. I mean, *really* step up. I had to be efficient, competent, and cheerful. I had to be good at my job. Better than good. Tonight, I had to rise to the cream of the waitress crop.

And I had to be totally objective about the whole thing.

This all was definitely going to go down the tubes faster than a fallen soufflé.

Positive thinking, I instructed myself firmly. *Raindrops on roses and red sour jacks and other things that are the opposite of doom and disaster.*

I pasted the brightest smile I could onto my face and perky'd my way over to my mother's—I mean, *Audrey's*—table.

To her credit, my mom didn't even flinch when she saw me. It had to surprise her to find me here.

"Hi there, how are you tonight?" I asked.

"Great, thank you," she said pleasantly. As if this entire exchange weren't surreal enough, she'd managed to disguise even her voice, drawling in a slow, steady tone that sounded nothing like my actual mother. I suppose that should have helped me to disassociate; instead, it freaked me out. Where was that dry-goods pantry rift in the time-space continuum when you needed it?

"Would you like to hear our specials for tonight?" There was no going back. I had to keep moving. I was like a shark. A shark wearing lime-green Pumas.

"That would be lovely," she replied.

I looked down at my pad, where the specials should have been written. They weren't there. I must have ripped the top sheet off my pad earlier. How? Why?

I paused. "Let me just go check on those

for you, okay?" I was almost proud of myself. From the tone of my voice, you would never even have known that I was rapidly melting into a cold little puddle of chocolate pudding.

"Sure. Oh, and actually"—she held out her water glass brightly—"if I could maybe get another glass that's clean?"

I leaned forward to inspect hers. Sure enough, it was adorned with greasy lipstick prints along the rim.

I struggled not to react to the big-time grossness of her water glass as I took it back from her.

"Of course," I said, smiling like I'd been hit with a dose of horse tranquilizers. I was a Stepford waitress. I was feeling no pain. "Just a moment."

The specials were stone crab claws served in a fennel consommé, braised short ribs, and a dark chocolate espresso mousse. Audrey decided to try them all (I had insider knowledge that she had tried all the signature dishes on her first visit), and I tossed a sprig of fresh parsley in her soup in a shameless attempt to score a few extra points.

Now, you know I wasn't thrilled to be at work on a night as busy as this, and it would not be untrue to add that waiting on my costumed mother was terrifying on the level of being asked to deliver an oral presentation in class stark naked. But I have to say, once I got over the initial shock of seeing Mom spackled in clown makeup, I got things together pretty quickly. I found her a sparkly clean water glass, I opened a bottle of wine for her without sending the cork shooting across the room or smacking myself in the chin with the corkscrew, and I even poured the fennel consommé from a mod little blown-glass pitcher into the bowl of stone crabs without depositing a single drop into my mother's lap.

Yay, me. With any luck, I could count on a decent tip from Audrey. Seeing as how we were blood relatives and all.

It wasn't until we got to the dessert course that things began to unravel.

Dark chocolate espresso mousse. I mean, yum, right? It's chocolaty, it's creamy, and it's got a sugar level that'll send you bouncing off home. If you liked chocolate, and you liked coffee (which my Energizer Bunny mom really, really did), it was clearly the way to go.

It was 10:13 when I took the mousse over to Audrey's table. I knew this precisely because I had been checking my watch feverishly ever since I'd sent Seth sprawling three hours before. From the moment I'd bodychecked the like of my life, and all throughout a meal that was totally formative as far as Hype's reputation was concerned, all I'd thought about was making it through the shift.

And I had. After my first two fiascos, I had. I'd gotten everyone's orders right, I hadn't spilled drinks, I hadn't neglected anyone's table for too long. I smiled. I cleared efficiently. I remembered the specials.

Yeah, I'd done all that—especially the specials. After choking at Audrey's table, I'd learned the specials upside down, inside out, and down cold. I even knew down to the millisecond when the kitchen had served the last stone crab.

But what I hadn't done was learn the individual ingredients in all the dishes.

"Here's your mousse," I said brightly, laying my mother's dessert in front of her with its accompanying porcelain bowl of old-fashioned whipped heavy cream. I smiled beatifically. She thanked me.

And took a bite.

When the mousse hit my mother's oh-so-sharpened palate, the reaction was instantaneous. Her eyes half closed and she smiled, even through her mouthful. Her entire face seemed to relax, and she gave herself over to what I knew had to be complete decadence.

And then, suddenly, she sat up straight.

A flush began at her throat and crawled its way up her neck. Her eyes began to water. She coughed, first softly, and then with increasing force. She bent over the table, bracing against it with her palms. Her chair rocked.

People were starting to stare, though for once, I couldn't care less. But given the circumstances, it was not a particularly refreshing change of pace. Had I poisoned my mother?

For the second time that evening, I froze. My mother. Was choking. At Hype. In a fright wig. Which was starting to slip off of her head.

This was a vortex of wrongness. There was no more wrong this moment could be. I closed my eyes to steady myself against a wave of nausea.

"Laine!"

It was Seth, proving yet again that he was way quicker on his feet than I was. He dashed toward my mother with a pitcher of water. He refilled her glass and crouched down next to her.

"Are you choking?" he asked.

She shook her head, still heaving fitfully. He pushed her water glass toward her, and she took it gratefully. He patted at her back while her coughs died down to a low sputtering.

It was like someone had pressed the play button on the DVD player. I darted to her side.

"Mom?" I asked, my voice sounding foreign and quavery to my own ears. "Are you all right?"

She gulped at her water glass.

"What was in the mousse?" she asked, her voice raspy and unsteady.

I shook my head in utter ignorance. "Chocolate. Espresso. Moussey things?"

I heard a throat clear and looked up.

It was Seth's father. A mix of emotions played across his face. None of them looked very warm or fuzzy.

"Ah," he began tentatively, "there was also some ground hazelnut."

Hazelnut!

Like, the one thing in the world that my mother was allergic to. One bite was fine, if uncomfortable and embarrassing. But if she had eaten any more of that mousse? The vortex of wrongness would have threatened to swallow Hype whole.

I felt faint again. I *had* poisoned my mother. For real.

At her job. At *my* job.

Oh, boy.

Slowly, my mother stood up from the table and stretched. She reached up with resignation and pulled her wig off of her head, running her fingers through her hair to shake it out.

Impulsively, I threw my arms around her.

"I'm so sorry," I murmured, my face pressed into her neck. "You know that was an accident."

Understatement. A massively, gigantically, overly understated understatement.

She leaned down and kissed the top of my head.

"Of course, Laine. It's okay." She rubbed at my shoulders. "I'm okay."

"Um, Laine?"

I looked up to find Seth peering at me in confusion.

"This is your mom?"

Um, yeah.

I could see where he'd be perplexed, seeing as how I'd spent half the evening catering to my mother without acting as though I'd ever met her before. My mother who happened to be dressed like a runaway circus freak.

Yeah, that might seem a little strange to someone who wasn't clued in.

But before I had a chance to explain, Seth's father stepped forward. With a look of wary recognition, he extended a hand to my mother to shake.

"Madison Harper?" he asked, his voice betraying his disbelief.

Seth's jaw dropped open. He whipped his head around to gape at me.

I couldn't bear the weight of his gaze. I dropped my eyes to the ground and refused to look up.

My mother smiled, straightened her shoulders, and reached out to take Seth's father's hand in her own.

"Hi," she said. "Yes, I'm Madison Harper, from the *Philadelphia Tribune*."

⭐

Anna: So you were outed?

Me: I am Outtie McOutterson, Queen of Outterdonia. *Everyone* at Hype knows who my mom is now.

Anna: Hmm. That can't be such a good thing.

Me: On a scale of one to ten? It rates about a negative thirty. When my mom shook hands with Seth's dad, that was, like, the worst moment of my life.

Anna: Worse than when you served your mom allergy pudding?

Me: The second worst moment of my life.

Anna: What did Seth say?

Me: *(long pause)* It wasn't so much a sentence, as an astonished stare, followed by unintelligible mumbling. Then he ran away.

Anna: (longer pause) Ouch. Awkward.

Me: Yeah, and after my mom left, Seth's dad had a little talk with me.

Anna: About your mom?

Me: More about the fact that I almost

killed her. And tackled Seth earlier that night. Um, he seemed a little bit bothered by those things.

Anna: Do you still have a job?

Me: Barely. I promised to shape up. What I *don't* have is any chance with Seth, ever.

Anna: *(taking a deep breath)* Well—

Me: Now would *not* be the time to remind me that I never had a huge chance to begin with. Or that I recently swore off love in the first place.

Anna: Check. What about backup boy, then? You should go for Damien. You deserve a fun night out, at least. Get your flirt back on, even temporarily.

Me: About that . . .

Anna: *What did you do?*

Me: *(defensive)* Nothing. I literally did nothing. After my mother left and I talked to Seth's father, I ran to the dry-goods pantry and hid. After his shift, Damien found me slumped against an economy-sized sack of steel-cut oats.

Anna: Which always says "romance" to me.

Me: Yeah, well . . . shows what you know. We're going for coffee tomorrow. The catch of the day has been reeled in.

Anna: *(unironically)* Yay!

Me: What can I say? He caught me when I was weak. I had no powers of resistance.

Anna: Resistance, schmesistance. Have fun. Only . . .

Me: What?

Anna: Stay away from the espresso and the hazelnut, babe. Just, you know, until you get your mojo back.

Thirteen

With Seth out of the picture, I was free to crush away on Damien with my typical flightiness. In all honesty the fling thing had lost some of its allure, but a girl can only spend so much time with a notebook and a highlighter pen. So when the time came for our date, I tried to psych myself up.

When Damien said that we were going for coffee, I sort of thought he meant we'd have some casual, froufy, bazillion-calorie concoction at a local Fourbucks franchise or something like that. But when he called me Sunday afternoon to finalize the plans, he explained that what he'd really had in mind was a dim, darkened, beatnik-y coffeehouse called Uncommon Grounds that he and his college friends frequented. I'd heard about it, but seeing as I was still in high school, I'd never been inside.

I was up for it, though. The last few adventures I'd embarked on—teaching cooking class, waiting tables, crushing on Seth—had yielded mixed results. I wasn't exactly hungry for adventure—I was way too depressed for that. But, you know, I was sort of . . . peckish.

I wasn't sure what to wear for a date with a college guy, so I decided on a fail-safe black tank top and jeans. It was the closest I had to poetry-slam clothing, and it seemed like this coffeehouse was poetry-slam territory. A little sheer lipstick, some hair wax, and I was possibly even looking a full six months older.

Damien had insisted on picking me up at my house. I figured it couldn't hurt. I wasn't hiding anything anymore, that was for sure. Not that my mother was even home. She was off terrorizing some other waitress with her bottomless bag of alter egos.

He said he'd come by at 7:00 p.m., and at precisely 7:02 our doorbell rang. Points for punctuality. I grabbed my most adorable, date-y bag and headed out the door to meet him.

"Hey," he said, smiling when he saw me. "You look great."

It's amazing what a little sheer lipstick can do for a girl.

"Thanks," I said. "You look . . . different when you're not behind a bar."

It was true. As we walked down my steps and then down the street, I realized that there actually wasn't any awkwardness to seeing him outside of work. It was like some small cocoon had burst open. Maybe I looked weird without an apron tied around my waist or a huge sauce stain creeping down my shirt. But we were more than just coworkers—we were obviously both practiced in the art of flirtation. After all the weeks of denying my feelings for Seth, it was kind of a relief to let my inner sex kitten out of her cage for an evening.

"I'll take that as a compliment," Damien decided.

College guys. They're so mature.

The coffeehouse was on the other side of town, near the university, but since it was a nice night and not too sticky, we had decided to walk. I was slightly out of practice when it came to witty banter, so I let him lead the conversation. The more he talked, the more I realized how little I actually knew about him.

Damien was from South Jersey and had spent his whole life there; it was a foregone conclusion that he'd stick around for college. He was following in his older brother's footsteps in where he went to school and even by tending bar to help support himself. I decided there was a certain comfort in that sort of easygoing, steady-Eddie approach to life. Probably. I mean, if my mom had been more steady Eddie and less career monster, maybe my dad would have stuck around, right?

He stopped in front of the entrance to the coffeehouse and pulled the door open for me.

"Ladies first," he insisted, eyes twinkling.

Once inside, it took my eyes a moment to adjust to the light. Or rather, the total lack thereof. It was about seven-thirty on a summer Sunday in Philadelphia—light was not in short supply outside. This place was obviously working hard to cultivate a bohemian vibe. Everywhere I looked, I saw worn, knotted wood, rickety chairs, and unadorned tables. An abandoned stool and a microphone stand stood pushed along the far wall.

Oh, I was *so* right about the poetry slams.

"Have a seat. I'll get us coffee." He patted me on the shoulder and pulled a chair out for me at one of the empty tables.

I settled myself in and surveyed the crowd. There were a few people huddled at tables by themselves, clearly students, tapping away at laptops and exuding a vibe of low-level pressure. One or two couples looked like they could be on dates—girls and guys leaning toward each other and speaking in hushed, intense tones. Then again, who knew if that meant a date? Everything about this place sort of screamed "intense." Maybe that was just a prerequisite for patronage.

"Here we are." Damien handed me a mug of steaming black coffee and tiny packets of creamer and sugar before easing himself into the seat across from me.

I emptied three creamer packets into the mug and stirred.

"I guess this place doesn't do mochas?" I smiled, trying to be a good sport, but the truth was that full-blown coffee coffee kind of makes me want to yak.

"Oh, uh, yeah," Damien said, still grinning. "Only one thing on the menu. A real coffeehouse, true to its name. You don't find many of those these days."

"So you're a purist?" I probed.

"I really am," he admitted. "What can I say? I believe that coffee should be made of coffee, that food should pick a cuisine and stick to it, and that smoothies are not meals. I guess I'm kind of old-school about stuff like that."

I pinched my thumb and index finger together in front of him. "Little bit."

My mother would have a field day with a guy like this, I realized. She was all for authentic, rustic flavor, but that was no reason to turn your nose up at everything new and experimental.

Damien was a guy, I suspected, who would never want to find any pesto in his lasagna. Or hazelnut espresso in his mousse.

"What are you doing working at a place like Hype?" I asked, frankly curious.

"Are you kidding?" He arched an eyebrow. "That bar is the best racket it town. New restaurant, downtown address, fusion cuisine . . . You've seen how busy we get."

I nodded. That was certainly true. Lukewarm reviews and my own iffy service be darned.

"Anyway, my brother always told me to go where the money is," he finished.

I could relate to that, obviously.

He leaned back in his seat and surveyed me quizzically.

"The question is, what are *you* doing working at a place like Hype?" he asked. "I mean, no offense, but since—"

"—since I'm the worst waitress in, like, ever?" I filled in for him.

He bit his lip. "Maybe not *ever*."

"But maybe," I agreed. I owned up to my sheer mediocrity when it came to waiting tables. I hardly had any other choice, by now. It wasn't exactly a secret, my suckiness.

I sighed. "I guess I was never really cut out to be a waitress. There are too many components to the job that are out of your control. But when Seth told me about the opening, I couldn't pass it up."

"For the money," Damien supplied, nodding.

Well, sure, for money, of course. Those lavender suede sneakers I'd seen at Target the other day weren't going to come marching to my house all on their own, after all. And, of course, I had visions of Ivy dancing in my head, and as we've discussed, Ivy doesn't come cheap. But it was definitely more than the money, and I knew it.

It was also Seth.

In some ways, Seth was pretty similar to Damien, I realized. I mean, he liked to follow recipes to a *T*, and he wasn't big on random experimentation. Unlike Damien, however, he was demonstrably impervious to my questionable feminine wiles. Both were totally hot, totally friendly and adorable guys. And Damien was exactly the sort of summer crush I would have lusted over this time last year.

But Seth—rigid, rustic, black-coffee-drinking Seth—was still the tastier choice to me.

Damien was charming with a capital "ch," but there was no denying it: Tiny little tasting menus just didn't appeal to me anymore. I was ready for a more substantial meal. If love was some kind of master menu, I decided, then Seth and I were decidedly different entrées. Seth was a roast chicken while I was wild game. Seth was cheeseburgers while I was teriyaki beef wraps.

Seth was chocolate and I was peanut butter.

We were different, but meant to be together. Of this I was sure. I'd swear on my *Joy of Cooking*.

I didn't share any of my culinary revelation with Damien—that would have been a flagrant violation of the rules of flirting. But I think that somehow, he could probably see it on my face.

Damien walked me home at the end of the night, and I worried for a moment whether or not he would try to kiss me. For all my mad crushing throughout the years, the last time I'd been kissed full on the lips was in a summer camp spin-the-bottle fiasco that had made me sort of phobic about repeat performances. At my front door, he leaned forward.

And I swiftly turned, pecked him on the cheek, and darted inside.

Coffee was fine—strong and bitter, sure, but I could deal. But honestly? My appetite was starting to perk up.

I was getting hungry again.

"Okay, so if the garlic is beginning to brown, then we turn down the heat and add the carrots," I said, using the royal "we" in a vain effort to convince Cameron and Marci that they had as much control over the oven as I did (they didn't). Cameron dutifully stepped forward and tilted a bowl of cleanly diced carrots into the massive pot of gumbo we were cooking today. It wasn't exactly summer food, no, but it was pretty easy, with slightly less potential to cause a big squicky mess.

"Hey, Seth," I called out, "if you guys are done rinsing the beans, I think we're about ready for them over here."

I shot a quick sidelong glance in his direction; our shifts hadn't overlapped at Hype this week, so this was my first time seeing him since last Saturday night. Personally, I was trying to forget that last Saturday night had ever happened, and I was sort of hoping Seth would do the same. Unfortunately, I couldn't tell what Seth was doing, seeing as how, since class had begun, he'd been studiously avoiding my gaze.

Maybe *that's* what he was doing: avoiding me. Studiously.

Fab.

"Uh, sure," he mumbled, passing a colander filled with rinsed beans to Barrie and gesturing for her to take them over to me.

I coaxed all the various ingredients into the main pots and gave the three more responsible students spoons. "Stir occasionally," I instructed. They nodded solemnly and stood at an appropriate distance from the range tops.

For the rest of us, corn bread beckoned. I mean, it beckoned from a mix, but hey, it was Seth's idea, and I'd decided to take one for the team.

The impermeable sheet of awkwardness and tension between Seth and me was starting to suffocate me. I had to do something. I had to grab the gumbo pot by its burn-proof handle, so to speak.

"Um, Seth," I called, going for broke, "do you want to help me grab the corn bread stuff from the pantry?"

"Sure," he said quietly.

In fact, he said it so quietly that I had to strain to be sure that he'd answered me at all. He still wasn't looking at me. I don't think anyone, in my life, had ever not-looked at me as aggressively as Seth was right now.

I gave the class one last once-over to be

sure that everyone was busy at some non-sharp, nonburn-y, nontoxic task, and, satisfied, headed off in search of corn bread mix.

The pantry was nothing like the enormous silo found at Hype; instead, it was more of a glorified closet. Quarters were a bit tight for two people who were working so hard not to look at each other that they were going to set the floor on fire with the strength of their averted gazes.

I stood on my tiptoes and pulled down two boxes of mix, a box of powdered eggs (gross, but they keep for much longer than fresh ones), and a huge vat of economy-sized vegetable oil. Seth was there to help me, of course, but seeing as how we weren't really speaking to each other—more like around each other—I was kind of wary of loading him up like my personal bellhop.

Unfortunately, there was no way I was getting all that stuff back into the kitchen myself. I struggled, but it wasn't happening. As I moved away from the shelves, I reeled backward, dropping all three corn bread mix boxes on Seth's foot in rapid succession.

"Ow, ow, ow," he said robotically, as each one smashed his toes.

"Sorry." I cringed and reached down to pick them up.

However, Seth had already crouched down to pick up the boxes. My own leaning down had the unfortunate effect of depositing the remainder of the packages directly onto his head.

The vegetable oil was the worst. The plastic made a twanging sound as it bent in and back out again. The vat bounced off the top of Seth's head and rolled noisily away. It banged against the wall of the closet and stopped, mercifully.

"I swear, I'm not trying to kill you," I gushed. "I just have, um, butterfingers. Or, uh, vegetable oil fingers."

It was a horrible joke, the kind my pun-loving grandfather would make. And also, I had given the boy of my dreams a baking supply concussion. Joking was perhaps not as useful right now as, say, running for the first aid kit would be.

Still, for a moment I saw the corners of Seth's mouth turn up as though they were headed in the general direction of a smile. But just as quickly as the expression bloomed, his face went stony and impassive again.

"I'm fine," he said.

"Good," I replied hastily. "But . . . is something else bothering you?"

Something other than the fact that I kept from you my mother's high-profile job and basically sabotaged her visit to your father's new restaurant? Oh, and that I also just brained you with three tons of unsaturated fat?

"I'm fine," he repeated, which didn't feel like the complete and honest truth. But what could I do?

"Okay," I said shortly, gathering together half of the supplies and wisely letting Seth carry his own load this time.

The door to the closet was ajar, but only slightly. I had reached with my free hand to push it farther open when I heard Seth clear his throat nervously behind me.

"So, ah, what'd you do last week, Laine?" he asked. "After I saw you, I mean."

Right, *after* I made a total ass of myself at Hype.

"Um, not much," I said, my face coloring. Just the memory of last Saturday night was excruciating.

It was true; after my ill-fated shift, the week had been relatively uneventful. Seth didn't want to hear about my Spanish translation tapes or my research into the local animal rescue organization. Or that Anna and I had tried Crest Whitestrips and decided we didn't like the way they made our teeth tingle. So that was a bust. And I'd reacquainted myself with my favorite books about girls sharing jeans and learning, growing, and etc-ing over the summer (their lives were *much* more eventful than mine).

And then there was the date with Damien. But I sure wasn't going to mention *that*.

"Huh," he said, shrugging his shoulders. "That's funny; I heard you went on a date with Damien."

I stopped in my tracks. How would he know that I'd gone on a date with Damien? My mind raced; had Damien told him? And if so, *what* had Damien told him? That I looked cute without my apron on? That I preferred to drink coffee when it was disguised as hot chocolate? That I was too immature to even kiss a cute guy (albeit one I wasn't that into) on the lips? What did boys talk about when they discussed these sorts of things?

More important, if Seth knew that I had

been on a date with Damien, did that make him want me more? Or less? Inquiring minds *needed* to know.

"Callie was saying. I guess Damien said something to her," Seth said finally, apparently choosing to ignore my sudden inability to communicate verbally.

So Damien said something to Callie? And Callie said something to Seth? This little chain of gossip (was it gossip if it was actually true?) had taken a different path than I would have anticipated. That probably meant something.

It's just, I had no idea what.

"Come on," Seth said, juggling his packages and making his way back to the kitchen tables. "Corn bread."

Right, of course. Corn bread.

Yum.

Fourteen

I had kind of thought that having things so weird and hopeless with Seth, with no sign of any other crush-y prospects on the horizon, and an incredibly tenuous grip on my own employment (not to mention my sanity) was sort of rock bottom. I'd thought that, short of learning I'd developed a late-blooming deathly allergy to mint chocolate chip ice cream, things couldn't possibly get any worse.

Alas, I thought wrong.

I was up bright and early Monday morning. This in itself was annoying; I didn't have to be at Hype until six o'clock, and there was no earthly reason to be awake before noon.

I tossed and turned in bed for almost an hour, trying unsuccessfully to fall back asleep. Nothing doing. Every time I closed my eyes, all I saw was Seth: Seth lying flat on his back at Hype, covered in the contents of his tray after I'd sent him sprawling; Seth saving my mother from a coughing fit and in the process learning more about me than I'd ever wanted him to know; Seth dodging rogue dry goods in the rec center pantry with me.

Seth knowing all about my date with Damien, and not seeming to care one way or the other about it.

When the summer began, all I'd wanted was to raise some money for college and boost my transcript. If I got lucky, something else would happen, too—a new adventure, a chance to try my hand at a new hobby, or an opportunity to meet people I didn't already know from high school. Maybe even all three at the same time.

I'd succeeded at that, of course: I started cooking, started teaching, and even started dating. I was okay—even pretty good—at cooking, and the truth was, I knew I was a decent teacher, too. When the kids weren't pelting me with various foodstuffs, I was pretty fond of them. So I had my whole roster set up. It was only my love life that seemed to be back-burnered. If my experience with Damien was anything to go on, I was kind of a lousy date. Or maybe I was just a one-guy kind of girl.

Even if that guy and I weren't dating, flirting, or really even talking to each other. Even if that one guy wouldn't look me in the eye.

Meanwhile, we won't discuss Misadventures in Waitressing.

But lying in bed was not improving my mood. I needed to motivate. Maybe some sugar cereal would help. I was a big believer in the healing powers of Cinnamon Toast Crunch.

I hoisted myself out of bed, shrugged a short terry-cloth robe over my tank top and shorts, and padded my way downstairs and into the kitchen. On autopilot, I shuffled to the fancy-schmancy coffeemaker my mom had been given as a congratulatory gift from her boss when she'd been promoted. I poured in the requisite ingredients and hit the button for a latte. So what if I liked my coffee dressed up a little bit? I was a woman—er, a teen—of complicated appetites, darn it.

While the machine went through its

elaborate hissing and sputtering process (I really had no idea why the creation of a latte involved more noise pollution than a demolition derby, but whatever), I settled myself casually against the kitchen counter by the morning papers. We had them all delivered, since my mom is predictably obsessed with her competition. The *Inquirer* had already been dissected and thumbed through, since my mother is *also* predictably insane and wakes up in the sixes— the sixes!—to get herself to work for a nice, eleven-hour day.

Normally I don't read the paper; as I may have mentioned, I'm more *People* magazine than politics. The closest I really come to issues of the day is when I watch *The Daily Show* with Anna, but that's maybe because I have a secret (or possibly not so secret) crush on Jon Stewart.

But, as usual, I digress. I took special notice of the paper this morning, once I realized that the Lifestyles section had been pulled, folded, and otherwise man—or Mom—handled.

Remember that I'd been hoping things couldn't possibly get any worse for me?

Yeah, that dream was dead.

WHY ALL THE HYPE?

The words screamed up at me in two-inch-high, boldface type. They couldn't have been more glaring if they'd been printed in neon green and glittered like a disco ball.

She'd done it. She'd visited Hype for the third time. Lord knows what costume she'd used this time, seeing as how the staff was kind of on to her these days, but she'd made it in on a night when I wasn't there, the one advantage to my shifts being cut back last week. And she'd written and run a review.

A really, really bad review.

No wonder she hadn't told me. She knew I'd freak out, and she didn't want to put me in a difficult position. Or a more difficult position that I'd already be in, seeing as how her cover—and therefore *my* cover—was already pretty well blown.

How could she not have told me?

A rush of dizziness engulfed me. This was bad.

Breathe, I commanded myself. I inhaled, but my breath came in quick bursts that only made me more lightheaded.

Okay, strike breathing, I decided, pulling

out a chair and settling shakily into it. *Let's think damage control.*

Option 1: The article wasn't really as bad as I was imagining.

I glanced at it again.

> On a given night, the new, loudly hyped (and appropriately named) fusion restaurant downtown is packed to the rafters with Philadelphia's high-earning, well-heeled recent grads. One can hardly blame them for this lapse in discerning taste. They're too young to know any better. . . .

Oh no, it wasn't as bad as I was imagining. It was way, way worse. The article went on to pick apart the restaurant in excruciatingly thorough detail. The food was mediocre, the menu was schizophrenic, the service was inattentive (thanks, Mom!).

Oh, it was all true.

And it was totally going to ruin if not my life, then at least my immediate future.

Option 2: Seth's father hadn't seen the article.

Unlikely. Even if he hadn't seen it yet,

there was no way he'd miss it completely. Like every other would-be restaurant mogul in the city, he read the papers religiously. They, too, are predictably obsessed with their competition.

(Note to self: Being a professional adult is competitive. And also? *Hard.*)

Option 3: Seth's father had seen the review, but Seth didn't care, because he was madly in love with me.

Beyond unlikely. This verged on *Lord of the Rings*–level fantasy. Of course Seth would care about the review. It was a massive trashing of his father. If Seth weren't the kind of guy to care about that, then he wouldn't be the kind of guy I'd be crushing on.

And as we know, I was still, however ill-advisedly, crushing on him, big-time.

If Seth read the review and didn't care that it had been written by my mother, well, then that only served to prove that he didn't care . . .

. . . well, that he didn't care about *me.*

I had to face facts: No matter how you sliced it, it looked like romance was off the menu. For good.

★

My bad mood, a kicky blend of grumpiness mixed with bona fide anxiety, intensified throughout the day. Anna wasn't available for a BFF consult, and talking to my mother wasn't an option. She was off in Deadlineland, but even if she'd been around, she was The Enemy. There would be no solace in talking to her.

The worst part was, she was only doing her job. Even though doing her job equaled crushing my social and professional life, I understood why she'd had to print the article.

Sometimes, being patient, understanding, and mature really sucked. Like now-times, for example. Now-times, all I wanted to do was curl up into a ball and watch reruns of *The Naked Chef* on an endless loop. For once in my life I wanted to veg out—to *be* instead of to *do*. Jamie Oliver was frenetic and chatty; I was a useless blob of tapioca pudding.

By five fifteen I could procrastinate no longer: I was due in at Hype.

I really, really, *really* didn't want to go. But given my performance record up until now, I didn't think skipping my shift or calling in fake-sick would win me the title of Employee of the Month. Especially seeing as how I was hardly a contender as it was.

I dug up my least wrinkled work uniform and dressed quickly, not having the energy for things like sheer lipstick or hair product today. Who cared if my bangs were flippy and shooting in two different directions? Lunatic bangs were the least of my problems right now.

Yeah, lunatic bangs or no, my goose was totally cooked.

Hype at six o'clock was a different beast from the monster that kicked my butt for hours on end. Busboys leaned quietly at the side-station, refilling the salt and pepper shakers, rolling cutlery into freshly laundered napkins, and making sure the pitchers of tap water were appropriately chilled. When the restaurant was like this—devoid of customers, blanketed in anticipation—you could almost imagine that it would be a fun, interesting place to work.

Almost. I mean, come on—I knew better.

There was barely a murmur of notice as I walked through the front door; people who were involved with prep certainly weren't going to stop what they were doing for me. That was totally fine. I'd be more than happy to put off discussion of my mother and/or her views of Hype for as long as possible.

I kept my head down as I made my way to the break room. I guess I must have, at some point on my way in, applied my own set of mental blinders. This had seemed like a good enough idea at the time—head down, do your work, just turn each table mechanically until the shift is over—but it left me completely and utterly unprepared for what I was to come across next.

I opened the door to the break room and nearly passed out.

If I had opened the door to a room full of tap-dancing giraffes wearing bikinis, I couldn't have been more surprised. Giraffes would have been a welcome distraction. *This*, however, took the tiny shred of objectivity to which I clung this evening and did a Mexican hat dance on it until it was buried and fossilized deep within the ground.

Damien. And Callie. Were fully groping. On the break room table. *Groping.*

With the frenzied intensity of two drowning victims, they grabbed at each other and made out like it was their job. On the break-room table, where I'd scarfed down countless tuna salad bagels between shifts.

For the second time that day, I felt dizzy. I was going to pass out. I was going to pass out on the floor of the break room. Meanwhile, Damien and Callie would go on making out, and when someone finally came to find me later (Who would it be? My mother? Anna?), they'd realize I'd been here all along. My legacy would be that I had totally stalked Damien and Callie's makeout session. And I would be creepy. The creepy voyeur with the lunatic bangs who couldn't even pour tap water without screwing it up.

This could not be my legacy. No freaking way. I'd rather just be known as the lousy waitress whose mom gave Hype the culinary kiss of death. Right now that was the best I could hope for.

"Excuse me," I mumbled.

They both barely glanced up, but that was hardly the point. I rushed out of there like my lime green Pumas were on fire.

Pop Quiz:
You've just discovered that your not-ex, not-boyfriend, person-that-you-had-kind-of-decided-you-didn't-want-to-date-anyway was making out with your number one archnemesis, right in the very break room where you hid from your bosses at your high-stress job that you were never much good at. Who is the worst possible person to run into at that moment of extreme emotional frailty?

A) Your crush, who probably hates you with the fire of a thousand blazing SunChips

B) Your crush's father, who—bonus!—also happens to be your long-suffering boss.

Answer Key:
A and B!
Oh, that's right. This is the lightning round, after all. If you guessed correctly, feel free to go swan dive into a vat of spray cheese, 'cause it's only downhill from here.

I literally bumped directly into Seth (as you know I was ever so wont to do). He stepped backward and blinked at me, panic in his eyes, then mumbled something unintelligible and darted off.

Something told me he had read the review.

Worse than Seth's maximum-overdrive avoidance of me, however, was the fact that when he was gone, I was left all alone with his father.

Who did not, it must be said, look pleased.

He squinted at me and sighed heavily. "Laine," he began, almost sighing my name, "why don't we have a chat in my office?"

Chatting in the owner's office is never a good thing. In fact, in the month or so that I'd been working at Hype, I'd never been in the owner's office. One was only called in there for times of extreme praise or times of extreme discipline.

It didn't take a decoder ring to see which way this conversation would be swinging.

Mr. McFadden pushed the door open to his office and ushered me in.

Given the tone of the occasion, I guess I'd been expecting something more along the lines of the principal's office at school: an orderly clutter, offset by various inspirational animal posters, a personalized mug, and a mouse pad or two.

Not so much. Mr. McFadden's office was a cramped, dank, windowless cave covered from top to bottom in triplicate forms, order processing sheets, and schedules emblazoned with a rainbow of highlighter stripes. It looked like a war zone, and Mr. McFadden was the commanding officer of culinary affairs.

"Have a seat, Laine," he said, his voice low and almost kindly. He gestured to the one extra chair in the room, a spindly rolling desk chair that had clearly seen better days.

I perched cautiously on the edge of the chair and folded my hands primly in my lap. I channeled every ounce of emotional energy that I had into looking contrite and responsible, from my scary bangs to my bangin' sneakers, every bit the model employee.

Yeah, I don't think he was buying it.

"I'm sure you're not surprised to find that I've read this morning's *Tribune*," he began, busting the newspaper out of a stack of papers four feet high and unfolding it with a flourish.

"Right," I said, not daring to meet his eyes. "But—"

"Now, I know you didn't write this review yourself, and you can hardly be held responsible for it, when your mother was just doing her job," he continued.

I allowed myself a hopeful breath. Was it possible that everything was going to be okay?

"But, Laine, this is not about blame. It's about facts," he finished finally, after what felt like a lifetime.

No, it was not even remotely possible that everything was going to be okay.

The signs had been there all along, of course, bubbling away insistently on the back burner. But they couldn't be ignored any longer.

I was a tempest in a teapot, albeit a quirky teapot that some people found attractive. And that teapot had reached its boiling point.

Was I steamed? Sure. But what did that matter? I was too hot to handle. And you know what they say: If you can't stand the heat, get out of the freaking kitchen.

Fifteen

Me: *(sigh)*

Anna: You called me, sister. Are you just going to sit there on the line, taunting me with your heavy breathing?

Me: That's not heavy breathing, it's abject despair. Jeez.

Anna: *Abject* despair? Okay, back up. Let's look at this more objectively.

Me: Can we? Please?

Anna: Kill the sarcasm.

Me: Um, it's just, you want objective? Here's objective: *Objectively*, my boss— also known as the father of the boy with whom I'm dying to 'get cooking,' if you know what I mean—

Anna: I know what you mean. Now promise me you'll never use that expression again. Seriously.

Me: *(loudly)* My boss has decided that it would be best if I were to "pursue employment elsewhere." His words, not mine. In other words, I'm fired.

Anna: Which sucks, I know—but, Laine, you hated that job. And you were kinda bad at it.

Me: I love when you point that part out.

Anna: I am only working with what you told me. So the job sitch was not ideal. Now it's over. And you know what? In a couple of weeks we'll be back at school and you'll be glad that you don't have a job to worry about.

Me: No, I won't. I'll need to come up with another job. This was supposed to be my thing. My way to earn money. For college. And sneakers.

Anna: The job will come. For now, why don't you concentrate on an aggressive campaign of window shopping. You weren't making anything in tips, anyway. Right?

Me: Again, thank you for your undying support.

Anna: Let's take what we can get right now.

Me: Right. Because you know what I *can't* get? A boyfriend. The boy I sort of liked decided to hook up with Superskank, like, five seconds after our date—

Anna: Because you weren't into him and she was! Besides, you knew that was the kind of guy he was. You know— a flirt. A kindred spirit. He's like a shark that has to keep moving in order to survive. And you were just . . .

Me: Just say it. *I* was just *his* crush of the day. Fine. Let's all take a moment to savor the irony. Whatever. But does that mean I need a front-row seat to soft-core pornography?

Anna: *(rolling her eyes so loudly that I can hear it through my cell phone)*

Me: So Bartender Boy and Bitchy McSpray-Tan are off in la la land, and meanwhile, I can't even get my teaching partner to show up for our gig. Our gig!

Anna, he skipped class this week.
I have driven him from class. I am
beyond a pariah—I am a menace to
the progress of preadolescent cooking
students everywhere.

Anna: Not everywhere. Just at the
Miles Halliday Community Center.
Miles Halliday was a strong man.
He'll bounce back.

Me: Do you even know who Miles
Halliday was?

Anna: Excuse me, but aren't we focusing
on your trauma?

Me: Right. So he skipped our class.
No word, no note, *nada*. Just me and
the kids.

Anna: *(gasping in shock)* How was *that*?

Me: I'm hanging up.

Anna: But I thought they loved you.
I thought you were, like, the student
whisperer.

Me: Don't try to change the subject.
The end-of-the-summer Halliday
carnival is here—

Anna: Fun for the whole family!

Me: *(forging ahead)* —and I had to come

up with what our booth would be, totally without Seth. What if he hates what we chose?

Anna: What did you choose?

Me: A pie-eating contest, but that's not the point.

Anna: That's *totally* the point. Who doesn't love a good pie-eating contest? Can you enter if you're over the age of eleven?

Me: *(tightly)* I will personally fill out your entry card if you will just admit that it's bad, bad news that Seth wasn't there.

Anna: It's probably not good news, that's for sure. *(pauses to consider)* But, you know, maybe it's got nothing to do with you. Maybe he was struck by, like, a flesh-eating virus or something.

Me: *(sighing)* At this point, I can only hope.

The last thing I wanted to do was to set foot inside Hype again, *ever*, but unfortunately, thanks to Seth's little disappearing act, I had to swing by and drop off the plans for our carnival booth. Halliday had people who were in charge of setting things up, but we'd have to bring our own materials—namely, the pies and a digital stopwatch.

The class and I had collectively (sans Seth, of course) decided to use store-bought pies only because we were pressed for time. I'd spent my last class with them—solo—hashing out flavors, rules, personal preferences, and other assorted nitty-gritty details. (Such as allergies. I had more than learned my lesson.)

Shockingly, we'd gotten through all the planning stages without Seth. But I still felt an obligation to be responsible. I had to fill him in.

Stupid responsibilities.

I came by on Sunday around two, when I knew the brunch crowd would be dying down. A quick glance around the joint told me that Seth was nowhere to be found. Did that mean something was wrong, and he hadn't been specifically avoiding me when he'd missed our class? Or did that mean he was going to incredibly extensive lengths to be sure he never ran into me again?

Maybe Seth was wasting away from avian flu or some other obscure disease I'd read about online. In which case, I would be kind of self-absorbed for thinking his absence had anything to do with me.

That said, if he *didn't* have bird flu, *he* was kind of immature for completely and totally hiding out on me.

Whatever. I still had the carnival to worry about, and if I kept up this psychotic obsessing, my brain was going to melt and dribble out my ears. *Highly* unappetizing.

The only person around, actually, was Damien. I hadn't spoken to him since his illicit lip-lock with Callie, and I wasn't too keen on adding another heaping dose of awkward tension onto my day. But what choice did I have?

"Hey, Damien, have you, uh, seen Seth around?"

He shook his head swiftly, seeming a scootch more comfortable with me than I was with him. Maybe he was extra-mature because of being in college and all.

"Nope, not yet. But according to the schedule, he's in later today."

Okay, then I needed to flee the scene as quickly as possible.

"Cool," I replied. "In that case, would

you mind giving him"—I dug into my tote bag and pulled out a sheaf of stapled papers—"these?"

I slapped them down on the bar and looked at Damien expectantly.

"No problem," he assured me.

"Great." I turned to go, but he reached out and tapped at my forearm.

"Laine—I'm sorry about what you walked in on the other day," he said, looking sheepish.

I waved my hand at him like it was no big deal. "I should have knocked."

On the door of the communal break room. Where you were getting inappropriately horizontal.

Whatever.

"Well, whatever. I mean, it's a public space . . ."

Thank you.

"But what I really meant was that it wasn't so cool for you to find us so soon after you and I went out."

No, no it wasn't. But . . .

Somehow, in the face of Damien's apology, I found myself able to just let it all go. What did it matter, anyway, if he'd turned out to be a little bit slimier than I thought? He wasn't my boyfriend, and he wasn't going to be my boyfriend. I knew what it was like to flit from crush to crush without ever letting yourself get really attached. It was easy. And usually fun. So how could I blame him?

And more than that, I realized with a start, I now knew, finally, that the person who *would* be my boyfriend would not be a making-out-in-the-break-room kind of guy. I could say that for certain, even though it was anyone's guess when the majestic day that person revealed himself to me would come.

Look at that: I managed to skirt my flirt rules for the summer, but over the course of two-ish months, I'd actually managed to juggle a big-old helping of teen-angst drama.

Yeah, so I hadn't gotten Seth in the end. That left a sour taste in my mouth. I thought he was special. Or possibly The One. He was my chocolate, after all. But it had all been experience that I could draw on as I went forward.

That sour taste in my mouth didn't have to be lemons, I decided. I could, if I wanted to, and if I concentrated very, very hard, make lemonade. Lemonade wasn't very . . .

sophisticated. But I'd have to make do.

"Don't worry about it," I said to Damien, shouldering my bag again and turning toward the exit. "We're good."

And with that, I walked out of Hype forever.

Sixteen

I decided to take Anna's advice about window shopping. Except, instead of window-shopping, I went shopping shopping. At the supermarket. For the ingredients for an apple toffee pie.

Why get store-bought for the carnival? I certainly had nothing better to do than bake away my misery.

On Wednesday afternoon I set about my pastry experiment. Pies were really not my forte. Thank goodness my mother wasn't around to see my early fumbles, such as a mountainous eruption of baking soda, some spilled milk (how clichéd), and an *eensy* issue separating egg yolks.

I'd clean it all up, anyway.

I was manhandling a mixing bowl when the doorbell rang, making me jump straight into the air with surprise. I certainly wasn't expecting anyone; Anna was working, and even if she hadn't been, she was terrified of me when I was cooking (I can be a little intense) and had learned, over the summer, to avoid my kitchen at all costs.

Imagine my utter shock to open the door to Seth McFadden.

Mmmmm.

"You . . . don't have bird flu," I managed to croak out.

He forehead crinkled. "Was I supposed to?"

"Uh, of course not," I said, blushing. "This is fantastic news."

"Great," he said briskly.

We both stood in the doorway for a moment more. I shifted my weight from one hip to the other. What was adorable Seth doing here? Why wouldn't he tell me what he was doing here? Was he dying of some other, nonavian wasting disease?

Unlikely.

But he still wasn't saying anything.

He coughed, making me jolt once again. I was a little bit nervous, having him in my house. I'll admit it.

"So . . . Laine?"

"Yep?" I asked brightly. Lord, I sounded like those customer service women from the computer call centers. "Yes?" I repeated, more evenly this time.

"Can I come in?"

Duh.

"Of course!" I said, nearly tripping over my own two feet to step backward and let him into the house. "Sorry." I beckoned him and we both hovered anxiously in the foyer.

"Listen, Laine, I don't know if you noticed, but I'd kind of been keeping to myself the last week or so," he began, sounding nervous.

Moi? Notice? Notice what?

"Oh, um, really?" I flubbed, shooting for "casual" and coming closer to "enormous spaz."

"Yeah, well." He fiddled with the zipper on his sweater. "I was being an idiot. I just . . . had no idea what to say to you after everything with our parents, and you, you know, leaving Hype and all."

He was an idiot? *I* was the one who couldn't carry a tray and a conversation at the same time!

"I mean, your mom was doing her job, and I get that that put you in a really weird position," he continued. "I would never have asked you to come to Hype if I'd known how uncomfortable it would be for you. And I'm really sorry if it didn't work out. I know my dad thinks you're great."

"Just not a great waitress," I quipped.

He tilted his head to one side. "Well . . ."

I laughed, letting him off the hook. "It's okay. We all have our special talents. I'm still trying to find mine."

His eyes widened. "You're kidding, right?"

"What do you mean?" I asked, baffled.

"Laine, you have a million special talents," he said. "I mean, when you cook, you're totally a natural. You know how to put your own spin on any recipe you try. I could never do that. In case you haven't noticed, I am obsessed with recipes."

He was being so gracious, I decided to let that one pass without comment.

But, amazingly, Seth wasn't even done yet. "And you're great with the kids at the rec center. Meanwhile, I spend most of the time trying to get Pete to stop giving me noogies."

"Yeah, he does seem to think of you as the younger brother he always wanted," I admitted, giggling.

"You're always fired up to go off in a million different directions," he finished, hooking his thumbs into the front pockets of his jeans. "You know exactly what you want, and you go for it."

"Do you know what you want?" Now I was back in banterland. This was familiar territory.

"I, uh, hope I do," he said, suddenly sounding more nervous. "The only thing I was worried about was that, well, I'd never be able to keep up. That's why, you know, I never said anything . . ." He trailed off uncomfortably.

"About what?" My heart raced and my palms were slick with sweat. Was this conversation going where I thought it was going? Had my crush du jour finally blossomed into a four-star relationship?

"About how I kind of liked you," he admitted finally.

"You kind of liked me?" I shrieked.

This was fantastic news. This was butter-cream icing on a devil's food cake. This was—

Oh, come on. This was way, *way* better than cake.

"Why didn't you say something?"

"I'm just a moron when I'm around a cute girl," he said, the tips of his ears turning fuchsia.

"Oh, well, in *that* case," I said, grinning broadly, "you're totally forgiven."

"Good," he said.

He leaned forward.

I squeezed my eyes shut in anticipation. This was totally it. This was my big, real-kiss moment. This was no summer crush; it was my full-blown, all-time, pretty-please-with-a-cherry-on-top fantasy come true in a monstrous, huge, super-sized way.

No *way* was I going to give him the cheek. Nuh-uh.

Seth paused suddenly and sniffed at the air.

"Uh, Laine?" he ventured. "I don't want to ruin the moment, but . . . do you smell something burning?"

Yeah, so in the end, we had to toss the first pie in the trash. But I didn't mind. That gave us a chance to start from scratch—together.

Once Seth and I had confessed our mutual crushage, we realized it was important to make up for lost date-y time. And what better place to turn up the heat than in the kitchen?

The end-of-the-summer carnival was a huge success, by the way. Our planning committee had done Miles Halliday proud, transforming the entire outdoor garden into a festive mass of balloons, colorful booths, and general mayhem and revelry. Seth and I manned the pie-eating booth until it was time for the contest, while the rug rats ran around wreaking havoc and generally making all the *other* instructors' lives difficult for a change.

As far as first dates went, it wasn't exactly conventional. But conventional is overrated.

Anna wandered by, sparkling with the creative stylings of the face-painting set.

"Hey," she said, leaning forward to investigate our selection. "Do you think I'll ruin my makeup job if I participate?"

"Without a doubt," I replied.

"Awesome," she said. "Sign me up."

I pushed the bright pink sign-up sheet toward her. "Sign yourself up," I chirped. "I'm on a date."

She rolled her eyes but picked up a Sharpie and scrawled her name with a flourish.

My mother, who'd taken a few hours off from her writing schedule to come out and support me, came up to the booth.

"Laine, I think there's a kid named Pete off terrorizing the ring-toss people," she informed me.

"Yeah, that sounds about right," I said. I wasn't going to let anything interfere with my good mood.

Anything, that was, except for Seth's father, whose shadow passed over us all at once, like a summer storm cloud.

Seth's dad.

My mom.

Me.

Seth.

Me and Seth.

Awkward.

Mr. McFadden cleared his throat. "Madison, hello. Good to see you again."

My mother's eyebrows arched slightly, as though she hadn't been anticipating a warm reception, but she eagerly jumped on the manners bandwagon.

"Likewise," she said warmly. "How is the restaurant doing?"

"To be honest," Mr. McFadden said, "it seems it's true that there really is no such thing as bad publicity."

"I'm glad to hear it." My mom smiled.

"And," he continued, "we've been lucky enough to come upon some very constructive criticism that I think will go a long way toward helping the place live up to its potential."

"Perfect," my mother said, and I couldn't have agreed more.

Behind my mother, Anna made a gagging face. I ignored her. Sticky-sweet adult etiquette was *so* preferable to the alternative.

Was it possible that we were going to all end up living (and cooking and eating) happily ever after?

"And Laine," Mr. McFadden said, turning back to me, "if you're still looking for a job, we've got a position open for a new hostess." He coughed discreetly. "It's a little less complicated than waiting tables."

Seth poked me in the side. "All you'd have to do is stand at the front door, looking pretty."

The gears of that big electric coffee grinder in my brain kicked into motion again. A job would be fun, and it would also mean more time with Seth. Besides, as a hostess, I didn't have to wear a uniform, and I could get cuted up every evening and strut around in sheer lipstick to my heart's content. My hair could show Callie's a thing or two, even if mine wasn't caramel colored. I could make some extra cash for college, too, seeing as how those waitressing tips hadn't exactly panned out.

"Excuse me," Anna said abruptly, stepping forward. "But no." She smiled at Mr. McFadden. "Thanks, but no thanks."

"Why 'no thanks'?" I asked, jolted from my sugar-plum dreams of tiptoeing through the two-tops like a floaty fairy hostess.

Anna managed to roll her entire body at me. "Laine, you just told me that you and Seth signed on for another semester of teaching the cooking class. After school, this time. *And* you told me that you would consider going out for the school newspaper this year—"

"Laine, sweetie, that's great news," my mom cut in, clearly proud that I was— maybe—following in her footsteps.

"*And*," Anna went on, ticking each point off on her finger as she made it, "it seems to me that you may have a few unforeseen social obligations cropp up in the immediate future."

She jerked her head meaningfully in Seth's direction.

He and I both had the good sense to look abashed, though I, personally, still felt pretty moony. I think Seth did too—in a boy way, of course.

I paused, considering everything Anna had said. I really took a moment to turn the ideas around in my head. I took one more deep breath and turned back to Mr. McFadden.

"She's right," I admitted. "It sounds great, and I really appreciate you thinking of me, but I just don't think it's going to work out right now. As much as I'd love to do it, the thing is"—I reached out and grabbed Seth's hand, and he gave mine a little squeeze—"right now, I think I've got more than enough on my plate."

Acknowledgments

Thanks to Michelle Nagler and Sangeeta Mehta for fabulous editorial expertise, Jodi Reamer for enduring my nervous breakdowns (emphasis on the plural), my brother David for loaning me his computer when mine was on the fritz, Noah for endless pep talks (and for stumbling his way through couples cooking class with me), Kathi Appelt and the faculty of Vermont College for kicking my butt (and expecting me to cite sources!), Aimee Friedman for letting me borrow her funny, and all of my extended family and friends, just because they're very extra awesome.

About the Author

Micol Ostow has always had a healthy appetite. At two years old she proclaimed a particular affinity for chocolate cake that persists to this day. She could cook up a fancy, multicourse meal if she wanted to, but since she lives in a Manhattan studio she mostly subsists on Doritos and gummy bears. Visit her at www.micolostow.com.

LOL at this sneak peek of

The Secret Life of a Teenage Siren
By Wendy Toliver

A new Romantic Comedy from Simon Pulse

⭐

"Roxy, you are a Siren."

"Come again?" I take the bow off my head, ripping out a few of my hairs. A few of my beautiful, shiny, straight, golden-red hairs.

"We're both Sirens."

"You can't be serious." I snort-laugh, sprawling out on my pillows. Did she get bitten by a rabid raccoon on the way here? A diseased prairie dog or a mosquito, perhaps? Or . . . is she telling the truth? After all, something very bizarre is happening here. Something I can't explain.

"Yes, honey. I'm serious."

"A Siren? You mean one of those mermaid things? If I jump in the water, will I grow a big fish tail?" I ask jokingly.

"Actually, the original Sirens had the upper bodies of beautiful maidens and the lower halves of birds. Through the ages, the image has evolved, and now Sirens are oftentimes depicted as mermaids. But we've evolved even further, and as you can plainly see"—she gestures up and down her pink-and-black Chanel suit—"we don't have any fish or bird body parts. Just beautiful woman parts."

It takes every ounce of self-control not to slap my forehead. What am I supposed to say, "Oh, that's cool. 'Cause I'm allergic to feathers, and scales don't do anything for my complexion"?

"So let's just pretend that we're having a completely sane conversation," I say when I finally find my voice. "I guess my next line would be something to the effect of 'Cool! I've always wanted to be an imaginary creature thought up by some dude in a toga.'?"

Sirens are imaginary, right? They aren't real. And I most definitely am not one. Feathers and scales aside.

She marches over to the bookshelf and slides out my Webster's. "Maybe this will help." Pacing around my room, she flicks through the pages and reads the definition out loud: "'Any of a group of female and partly human creatures in Greek mythology that lured mariners to destruction by their enchanting music.'" She shakes her head. "Here's another one. 'A woman who makes bewitchingly beautiful music; a temptingly beautiful woman.'" She taps her finger on the page. "Yes, yes."

As this is sinking into my mind, she sits down on my bed and gazes at me all mushy. Like how I'd imagine she looks at the puppies at the pet store. Or the lobsters in the tank at fancy restaurants. "My granddaughter is a Siren."

Oh, God. She's the portrait of sincerity. Grandma Perkins truly believes I'm a Siren. I swallow, contemplating what to say next. I guess I'll just go with the flow. Test the waters, so to speak. At least it'll make her happy. And maybe, when she comes back to the real world, we can just pretend like none of this happened.

"You didn't know until today?" I ask. "That I'm a Siren or whatever?"

Her green eyes twinkle. "I had my suspicions. You have so much beauty on the inside, you just needed for the outside to catch up."

"Why didn't you tell me?" I ask, lifting the leather-bound book onto my lap. "If I'd known I had even a chance of becoming knock out gorgeous, it would've saved me a lot of pain growing up. Do you have any idea how many times I've been called Pepperoni Face? Peppermint Patty? Band Geek of the Week?" I can go on and on. . . .

"I *couldn't* tell you, dear. It's one of the two rules. We cannot tell a soul. If we do, we lose our Siren powers. Of course, if you someday have a daughter or granddaughter who becomes a Siren, you can mentor her, as I'm doing for you." She rocks back and forth gently, a wistful look in her eyes. "My mother told me I was a Siren on my sixteenth birthday."

I never knew my great-grandmother, but I've seen pictures. She was one of the most elegant, beautiful women I've ever seen—sorta like Nicole Kidman but not as pasty. "So your mom was a Siren, then you . . . and now me? What about Mom?"

She leans in so close I can smell her minty breath. "The Sea Nymph gene is passed down from mother to daughter, but occasionally it skips a generation or two to help ensure that we're not discovered."

"Does Mom know you're a Siren?"

"No."

"Will she know *I'm* one?"

"I'll come up with a cover for your physical transformation, so don't worry about that."

This is ridiculous, ludicrous, *crazy*. And yet Grandma Perkins looks so serious and so . . . happy. What's the harm in playing along for a bit longer? "You said the first rule is we can't tell anyone. What's the other rule?"

She takes a deep breath and squeezes my hand so hard I swear she's cutting off my circulation. "A Siren cannot fall in love."

This is getting crazier by the minute. "Can't fall in love? Why not?"

She takes *The Siren Handbook* from my lap and flips the pages until she finds whatever she's looking for. In a reverent, almost musical voice, she reads: "'Once a woman becomes a Siren, she cannot fall in love. Whilst she can enjoy camaraderie and liaisons with the men she encounters along the journey of life, she is forbidden to bequeath her heart. Like the Sirens of Greek mythology, Sirens of today have irresistible yet deadly allure. If a Siren allows a man to get too close to her, he shall live just a moment more in pure ecstasy and then suffer a horrific, untimely death.'"

I peer at the book as she's reading, and,

like the title, there's just a bunch of mumbo jumbo swirled on the page. It's as if a two-year-old got ahold of her mommy's calligraphy pen and went to town. I snatch the book from her and flip through the pages. "How can you read that? What language is it in?"

"The Sirens of past all had musical gifts. One sang, one played a flute, and one played a lyre," Grandma Perkins says. "My gift is singing. When I want to use my Siren powers to their fullest, I sing." She bends over and picks up my flute case. "I suspect your musical gift is playing the flute."

"Contrary to what Mom says, I'm not very good. I mean, I sit in the third seat, but that's only when Macey McMullen's got a sinus infection."

"Play your flute, and the words will come to you."

"So if I just play a little song on my flute, I'll be able to make sense of these markings?"

"That's right." After Grandma Perkins closes the book, she takes my hand and looks into my eyes. "Honey, I know this is . . . quite incredible."

I spring up off the bed and twist open the blinds. Gray clouds are gathering in the otherwise blue sky. Grandma Perkins's sporty little Lexus is parked in the driveway. Seems like she's always got a new car. "Are there other Sirens out there?" Maybe there's a Siren chat room. Or a Sirens Anonymous chapter around here.

"We can't be sure." She joins me at the window and puts her hand on my shoulder.

Fat raindrops splatter rhythmically on the street. "Because we can't talk about it to anyone but each other," I say. Of course. And it's not like anyone would believe us anyhow.

Grandma Perkins says, "It's for your own protection, honey. If the word got out, you and I would become living science experiments."

"Or we'd be on the front page of the *National Enquirer*, along with the vampire sheep and woman who gave birth to triplet aliens," I say with a laugh.

Grandma shrugs. "You never know. That's why it's so important that we keep it a secret." She studies her appearance in my mirror and smooths her already perfect hair. Her eyes find mine in the reflection. "Now, you stay in here and learn about being a Siren. I'm going to start your birthday dinner." She gives my shoulder a couple of pats and then turns to leave.

This is all so ridiculous. I'm not a Siren. Grandma Perkins isn't a Siren. There are no such things as Sirens. Even the dictionary says they're some kind of creature from Greek mythology. They're not ordinary girls who go to high school in the Denver suburbs.

But how can I explain how I've turned from Plain Jane to drop-dead gorgeous in mere minutes? Unless my life has been one big Scooby-Doo cartoon and I've been wearing a band geek disguise for sixteen years, then maybe . . . possibly . . . *perhaps* there's a grain of truth to this whole Siren thing.

"Grandma?"

She turns around. "Yes, Roxy?"

"So, if I'm a Siren—"

"You *are*," she says softly.

I clear my throat. "So I'm a Siren and now what? I mean, what's the point?"

Her green eyes glow. "You've been given a gift, and how you use it is up to you. This handbook will help you answer your questions. And you can always come to me, Roxy. Anytime." She winks at me and then closes the door behind her.

Can this really be happening?

indie girl

a girl with a dream...
almost nipped at the seams!

a novel by Kavita Daswani

She's got what it takes. . . .

Indie Konkipuddi has always dreamed of becoming a fashion reporter at *Celebrity Style* magazine, so babysitting for publisher Aaralyn Taylor's son is *almost* her dream job. When Indie scores the juiciest fashion gossip in town, it just might be her ticket to a real internship . . . but will Aaralyn ever see her as more than the hired help?

FROM SIMON PULSE
Published by Simon & Schuster

Get smitten with these scrumptious British treats:

Prada Princesses
by Jasmine Oliver

Three friends tackle the high-stakes world of fashion school.

10 Ways to Cope with Boys
by Caroline Plaisted

What every girl *really* needs to know.

Does Snogging Count as Exercise?
by Helen Salter

For any girl who's tongue-tied around boys.

The adorable, delicious—
and très stylish—adventures of
Imogene are delighting readers
around the globe.
Don't miss these darling
new favorites!

by Lisa Barham

From Simon Pulse
Published by Simon & Schuster